The
SUMMER
HOUSE

PHILIP TEIR

*Translated from the Swedish
by Tiina Nunnally*

A complete catalogue record for this book can be obtained from the
British Library on request.

The right of Philip Teir to be identified as the author of this work has been
asserted by him in accordance with the Copyright, Designs and Patents Act 1988

F I L I FINNISH LITERATURE EXCHANGE

This work has been published with the financial assistance of
FILI (Finnish Literature Exchange)

The characters and events in this book are fictitious. Any similarity to real
persons, dead or alive, is coincidental and not intended by the author.

First published in Swedish as *Så här upphör världen* by Schildts & Söderströms
and Natur och Kultur, 2017.
Published by arrangement with Partners in Stories Stockholm AB, Sweden

This paperback edition published in 2019

First published in Great Britain in 2018 by Serpent's Tail,
an imprint of Profile Books Ltd
3 Holford Yard
Bevin Way
London WC1X 9HD
www.serpentstail.com

ISBN 978 1 78125 928 3
eISBN 978 1 78283 392 5

Designed and typeset by sue@lambledesign.demon.co.uk
Printed by CPI Group (UK) Ltd, Croydon CR0 4YY

1 3 5 7 9 10 8 6 4 2

THE BOY AND HIS MOTHER retreat to the car when the storm comes in. It's August. A green Toyota near the Finnish coast, parked on a hill in the woods. It's raining. The water makes furrows in the mud surrounding the car and runs down into the woods and the blueberry bushes.

The boy is thinking that his mother is making too much of things, that they're hiding out here because she likes adventures. They could just as well have stayed indoors to wait out the thunderstorm.

'The tyres don't conduct electricity,' says his mother. 'The safest place to be is inside a car. The tyres are made of rubber, you know. We'll sit right here until the sun comes out. It won't be long,' she says, even though he can see that the cloud cover is thick and grey. Impossible to see through.

He asks if they could listen to the radio. His mother hesitates, explaining that it might lead the thunder to the car, that it might entice the lightning to strike them. Then she switches on the radio.

'This is the safest place to be,' she tells him again.

She thinks he's scared of the thunder, but it doesn't really bother him. The lightning doesn't bother him either, or the rain out there, for that matter. All that water rushing around the car and through the mud.

He's thinking about something else. About what happened

when she was talking on the phone earlier in the kitchen. A shift occurred. He could hear it in her voice, in the way she answered. He could tell she was lying. He could hear it in her tone of voice, and it was as if he saw his mother in a new way. He knew that from now on, everything would be different. He didn't know how, only that things would not be the same. Something was going to change in their life, and change would make matters worse.

He'd been sitting behind her at the kitchen table while she cooked, watching as she intermittently picked up the mobile to check for something. He looked at her back, which was turned to him as she stood there in the kitchen and stared at the phone. Suddenly he could see it so clearly – the fact that she was her own person and not just his mother. In the way she moved he could see the person she had once been, her life before he was here. When she turned to him and smiled, he could see that she was worried, and he thought about all the things she might be worried about that had nothing to do with him.

But now the radio is on, and music is playing. She seems to be listening to the music. He looks at her and feels happy, so he listens too. Outside the rain is falling, but inside the car a moment still exists when everything is the way it used to be.

She leans forward to turn up the volume so the music drowns out the rain. And now the thunder returns: a dull rumbling somewhere beyond the chimney, up on the slope, away from the woods. It sounds as if someone is walking up there with a wheelbarrow full of rocks. That was what his maternal grandfather used to say jokingly: God is pushing a wheelbarrow full of rocks. And about the rain, he'd say: God is taking a piss.

He doesn't know how long they sit there, but he counts at least ten seconds between the lightning and the thunder.

Gradually the thunder fades, moving away towards the sea. His mother opens the door to go back inside the house, but the boy wants to stay in the car for a while by himself.

He turns off the radio and listens. Now all he hears is the sea a short distance away, a steady roaring sound. He opens the car door and gets out to walk down to the road, where he begins making big grooves in the soft sand. He makes channels for the water, which runs towards the ditch. He breaks off a piece of bark and lets it sail away.

He kneels down in the mud, feeling the wet sand between his hands and on his toes as the rain runs down his forehead.

That's when he sees the woman. Her feet are muddy, she has no clothes on. She walks stiffly along the road, moving past as if she doesn't see him.

part one

the family

1

JULIA WOULD TURN THIRTY-SIX in the autumn, yet she had never truly managed to escape her mother's voice. Even when Julia hadn't spoken to Susanne in a long time, her voice was still present, issuing at a high frequency and from up above – since her mother was a tall woman – and she always seemed to be in the middle of an opinion, in the middle of a statement.

'A person certainly doesn't have to shower me with praise for me to like her.'

'I've subscribed to that women's magazine for twenty years, and it's full of useless information, but I plan to continue reading it to the bitter end.'

'Have you put on weight? That's not meant as a criticism; your weight has always fluctuated a bit.'

Even now, as Julia sat in the tram on her way home from work, she could hear her mother talking in the back of her mind, rather like a verbal form of tinnitus, a constantly churning opinion machine. She could hear Susanne saying that she ought to write every day; that she needed to think up activities for the children (Susanne's repeated refrain was that Julia's kids seemed lethargic and didn't get out enough); that she needed to think about her career, the mortgage, her weight; but above all she ought to devote herself to Susanne, since Julia's mother considered herself to be the natural centre of the family.

Julia got off the tram, feeling as if she wanted to give her whole body a shake, the way a wet dog does when it comes inside. She tried to remind herself that her summer holiday was starting today, and she had all sorts of things to think about other than her mother.

She opened the door to the flat to find that no one was home. For a second she wondered if they'd left without her. Erik had said he would fetch the children at eleven, but she hadn't been able to get hold of him all day. The car should be already packed, and they should be on their way soon if they were going to get there by evening.

Julia wanted to air out the summer house and change all the bed linen before bedtime. She wondered whether they should give everything a good dusting as well, since no one had been out to Mjölkviken in a long time. Presumably she'd also have to scrub the refrigerator before they could fill it with food.

She rang Oona, who had been helping out with the children during the summertime weeks while she was working.

'No, Erik hasn't phoned. Should I send the kids home?' asked Oona. Julia could hear the sound of a piano in the background. It was probably Alice playing.

Oona, who was in her sixties, was from Estonia. She had moved to Finland long ago because of a man and now she lived alone. She had become a constant part of their lives, mostly by chance, because Alice had taken piano lessons from her, and Anton had occasionally gone to Oona's flat with his sister.

'Yes, do that,' said Julia. 'We have to leave soon.'

'Will you be away all summer?' asked Oona.

'We won't be home until early August.'

It struck Julia that she should have taken Oona a present. That was the custom when summer arrived. A tin of biscuits, a flower bouquet, or maybe several pretty ceramic cups made by Arabia. But Julia had never been the type to organise a collection for gifts for the children's teachers. She had always left that task to other parents. How was she supposed to know about such customs, let alone keep track of them?

She ended the call and tried to ring Erik. He didn't pick up, so she sat down on the sofa to wait.

Anton was the first to come in the door. He'd gained weight during the spring. It was as if his ten-year-old body was preparing for a growth spurt. The doctors had said he'd be even taller than his father, which was something he loved repeating to his friends. Anton didn't know that Julia sometimes eavesdropped when he invited friends home, but she did. She would listen to the ten-year-old boys trying to impress each other with all the things they thought they knew about the world.

'Have you heard anything from your father?' she asked.

'He phoned,' said Anton. 'He said he'd be home later.'

'So what did you do today?'

Anton shrugged. 'We played Monopoly. But Oona never dares take any risks, so I won both games,' he said.

'What did Alice do?'

His sister had now come into the front hall and tossed her jacket on the floor.

'She played piano and was really annoying,' said Anton.

Alice came into the living room without saying anything. She merely sat down on the sofa next to Julia, holding her mobile phone in her hand.

'Would you like to help me pack the car?' asked Julia.

'Do we have to?' said Anton.

She went out and drove the car up to the front entrance. The kids reluctantly helped carry the suitcases out, and the boot was soon filled.

When they were finished, Alice and Anton sat down on the sofa, keeping their shoes on, as if ready to leave at any moment. They asked their mother where Pappa was, and Julia told them he was still at work. It was the best answer she could come up with.

She asked the kids whether they were hungry.

'I'm not hungry. I want to get going,' said Anton. 'Why isn't Pappa home? I hate waiting.'

Anton threw himself sideways on the sofa, bumping into his big sister.

'Hey!' said Alice. 'Mamma, I can't stand listening to him whine. Anton, could you please shut up?'

Anton slugged her on the shoulder.

'Why'd you do that? Mamma, did you see what he did?'

Julia sighed.

'You're such an idiot,' said Anton, making a point of covering his face with his hands as he fell back against the sofa cushions.

Julia proceeded to clean the flat, trying to block out the sound of the children so as not to get annoyed. She scrubbed the bathtub, made the beds, and threw out all the food left in the fridge.

As she walked through the hall, she caught a glimpse of herself in the mirror, and was surprised to realise she looked good in a rather stern sort of way. So this was how a single mother looked, this was how she would look from now on, when they became a family of three. She went into the living room and sat down next to the kids, immersing herself even more in her fantasy.

'Want to show me what you're looking at?' she said to Alice.

'It's nothing.'

Julia leaned forward and looked. Alice was making a photo collage on her phone. There were three selfies, which she was turning into weird faces by swiping her finger under the eyes so the only thing visible was the whites of the eyes.

'Is that what you're all doing now?' asked Julia.

'I have no idea,' said Alice, shrugging.

'Why don't we take a selfie of the three of us?' Julia suggested.

'Mamma,' said Alice.

'Let me do it,' said Anton.

Erik came home at two, stressed and talkative, as if trying to avoid the fact that he was late. 'My mobile ran out of juice, and we had a meeting that went longer than expected. But I rang Oona to let her know. I wasn't sure when you'd get off work today.'

Julia sighed.

'I don't want to fight about this. I've packed up the car and cleaned the whole flat. I emptied the dishwasher and the fridge, and now I'm totally sweaty.'

'Does it really matter whether the place is clean when we get back?' he asked.

She was always struck by how real Erik was when he was at home, as if there were two Eriks: one she could be cross with in her fantasies, and a real Erik, who talked to her and had opinions that required her attention.

'Well, I suppose not, but we need to leave now if we're going to get there by evening,' she said.

'It stays light almost all night. It won't matter whether we get there at seven or nine,' he said, kissing her on the forehead. She accepted his touch with the sense of relief that comes from familiarity, a comfortable place where everything seems logical and simple because that's how it has always been. She pushed aside the ambivalent feeling of alarm and tension that still lingered inside her, a feeling that appeared whenever she wasn't able to get hold of Erik or she didn't know where the children were, a feeling she couldn't control because her thoughts were always going where they shouldn't. It was rather like dreaming in an awakened state; her brain was doing the work it really should be doing as she slept, processing the day, preparing for disasters.

They turned off the lights in the flat, unplugged the refrigerator, and checked one last time that nothing was switched on. Then they left. Anton jostled Alice as they went down the stairs.

Erik got into the driver's seat. He pulled out onto Manneheimvägen. The kids sat in the back, each with a laptop so they could watch films. Alice had been given some money to go to the shop to buy sweets and croissants for herself and her brother. Now she had them carefully lined up on the suitcase that lay on the seat between them. She would turn thirteen this summer and would soon enter secondary school. Then she would dress all in black and listen to music nonstop. Julia sometimes had trouble seeing herself in Alice, maybe because she'd grown up in a small town with mopeds and girls who used hairspray and secretly smoked behind the school building. An environment in which no one made particularly high demands of life, their plans often reaching only as far as the next weekend. Alice took everything much more seriously – school, her feelings, her style of dressing. It seems so much harder to be a child in this age of the internet, thought Julia, when everything has to be constantly documented and displayed.

The drive to Jakobstad used to take six hours, including time for breaks – they always stopped at the same place in Jalasjärvi – so Julia figured they should arrive around nine o'clock.

They had never stayed at the summer house before. It had stood virtually empty for the past fifteen years, up in the woods. It was a big, dark, timbered house situated a couple of hundred metres from the shore. Erik was the one who had finally persuaded her that they should spend the entire summer there, in spite of her objections. He had argued that the children had never had a proper holiday out in nature. Until now they'd always chosen to spend their summers in Helsinki or Stockholm, with only brief visits to Jakobstad.

'They need to get away from all these screens,' he'd said, and Julia had found it hard to argue with that.

The house was next to a small lake, or tarn, and was certainly big enough for their family. The ground floor had a living room, kitchen and bedroom. The kids would sleep upstairs in the attic. Julia's maternal grandfather had bought the place in the seventies when summer houses on the bay were still cheap and the Mjölkviken area was undergoing development, with newly built tennis courts and one-storey villas with big picture windows facing out to sea. It was a time when factory executives and middle-class families from the Ostrobothnian area of western Finland suddenly wanted to live as if they were on the Riviera.

Julia had written about the summer house in her first novel, titled *Mjölkviken*, which had been published five years before. It was the story of a young girl's summer days, largely based on her own childhood. The book had received fine reviews, considering it was a first novel. It had been quickly translated into five languages, and was nominated for the prestigious Runeberg Prize. Yet she had never spent any time in Mjölkviken as an adult. She'd made only one trip there in the wintertime, taking the children along to show them the house and the sea.

'Oh, it's great to be on holiday,' Erik said now. There was almost no traffic. Julia rummaged through the glove box for her sunglasses.

'It's important to make the drive at the right time,' said Erik. 'Everyone wants their holiday to coincide with Midsummer, but we're leaving the city early. The roads are practically deserted, and we'll be there in no time.'

Erik had saved up a few extra weeks of holiday, and they wouldn't have to be back in the city until school started for the children in August. Julia thought about that now: ten whole weeks. That was a long time to spend together. Only an hour ago she'd been imagining what it would be like to live alone with the children. Now, as she recalled that feeling, it seemed absurd. She looked at Erik and reached out to stroke his cheek.

'Wow, your hand is cold,' he said.

2

ERIK TURNED ON THE radio. He chose a music station because he didn't want to hear the news. The media should have picked up the story by now, and he didn't want Julia to ask any questions.

'Important meeting at 9.30.' That was what it had said in the subject line this morning when he checked his emails on his mobile. The email itself offered little information other than to say that the whole staff, except for the shop clerks, were to gather in the big conference room on the ninth floor. 'The meeting will be streamed on our internal network so those who can't join us physically will be able to participate.'

The room was packed when Erik arrived. It was 9.28 in the morning, and only a fraction of the staff had actually found seats at the conference table. Everyone else was sitting in extra chairs or leaning against the walls, like school children gathered for the morning assembly. Through an open window Erik could see central Helsinki. It was a beautiful, mild summer day in mid-June. The light and the bustle out on the street only emphasised the tense atmosphere in the conference room.

Yet there was also an underlying trace of sarcasm in the air. No one wanted to show any sign of anxiety about potentially negative news. By now humour had become a serviceable defence mechanism as their workplace was constantly being bombarded with bad news.

Acting upset or concerned about the business was not an option because that would mean positioning themselves on the side of their employer. Erik knew that no one in the room really believed anyone in management knew what they were doing. There were many who had differing views on how the department store could be better run. But these were views that were voiced in other settings, when the bosses were not present. For instance, over a beer in one of the restaurants on the other side of Mannerheimvägen.

Everyone knew that personnel costs were high. The internet was becoming dominant within the retail marketplace, and people often came into the department store to try on clothing or check out products they then purchased at home from various online companies.

'Can anybody tell me what's going on?' asked Mia, who had come in later than everyone else. She worked at the information desk on the second floor, and it was often her voice they heard on the store's loudspeakers whenever a customer needed to be paged. Everyone knew who Mia was: a mother of four with lots of energy and a perpetual tendency to turn up late for staff meetings.

Erik could see that Mia was upset, but no one dared answer her question. They merely shrugged.

'I don't have time for this. There's nobody covering customer service right now,' she said. 'If we're really concerned about how things are going, we need to start by making sure we're not understaffed on a Friday.'

'The situation's not going to improve,' said an older man. His expression was gloomy, his face almost grey, as if covered with a thin layer of dust. Erik recognised him from the food department on the ground floor. He could just imagine how the man had been planning every detail of his approaching retirement, and now he was envisioning his benefits evaporating.

The door opened and the boss came in. Her high heels struck five military taps on the floor before she stood at the head of the table.

'Thank you for attending this important meeting today on such short notice,' she began.

Riina Pitkänen had worked at the department store for only a year, and no one seemed to know anything about her personal life, although rumours had circulated about what she did in her free time. Erik's supervisor Jouni had suggested *Eyes Wide Shut* types of orgies, 'with whips'. Erik never took part in that sort of speculation because he had no patience for such chauvinist remarks.

Then again, one of the first changes Pitkänen had made was to eliminate an entire department devoted to fishing gear on the fifth floor in order to make room for more horse-riding paraphernalia.

Right now she was speaking in a way that made Erik think she was very nervous, as if she were keeping her voice as monotone as possible so as not to allow the slightest quaver.

Rumour had it that Riina Pitkänen had been hired to clean up the company's finances and provide guidance through the restructuring process facing the department store. Her background was in administering various Finnish foundations, and her achievements included instigating the unpopular merger of several local newspapers over the past few years.

For some reason Erik happened to think about a substitute teacher he'd had in primary school. All of the pupils had taken against her so vigorously that she had quit after only three weeks.

'I realise that not everyone is here. The sales clerks will be given the same information in written form,' Pitkänen was now saying.

'I've called this meeting today because I have both good and bad news. Let's start with the good. Well, I suppose it's no secret, since you've undoubtedly read the papers, that we're facing greater financial challenges than we have in many years. We've been fortunate and were able to show a relatively stable financial picture up until 2008, but since then things have changed.'

She glanced down at her computer, which apparently held notes for her speech.

'Of course we're not alone in our concerns about the situation, which has affected the entire retail market. We've managed to keep ourselves relatively afloat – and will continue to do so – largely thanks to an ownership structure that provides a good deal of capital. But right now the company is showing negative results that not even our owners can accept, and the deficits are rapidly increasing. For that reason, it is inevitable that something has to be done, and we've been looking at many different solutions. One thing is clear. We need to restructure this summer. You will be notified of the exact details in good time. It will take place over the next five weeks, and the great thing is that all of you will be invited to participate in the process. We're going to create various planning groups that will each provide input as to how it wants this department store to look, moving forward. Anyone who wishes to take part can join one of these groups. But let me say from the outset that working with a group does not guarantee you a future place with the company. However, the opposite is also true. If you decide not to participate in the planning sessions, this does not necessarily mean you will be let go.'

She concluded by speaking directly to the web camera positioned on the table.

'A press release has been sent to the media. If any journalists contact you, I ask you to make use of the information contained in the press release.'

'So what's the good news?' asked the man who worked downstairs in the food department.

'The good news? That's what I just told you. All of you will be invited to participate in the process regarding the reorganisation. You will all have the opportunity to make a contribution.'

It occurred to Erik that this was rather like inviting them in to plan their own funeral.

'How many people are going to be fired?' asked Mia.

'We expect to lose about one hundred full-time employees,' replied Pitkänen.

'My God, that's nearly a fifth of the entire staff,' said Kaj Forslund, a big bald man who worked in the warehouse. He had long served as head of the union, a role he took very seriously. Everyone trusted him because he seemed to know what he was doing, but above all because he belonged to the generation that was still passionate about union issues. Many of the younger employees came and went, without ever paying much attention to their employment rights.

'Yes, but we're hoping that a large percentage of them will leave with various exit packages. For example, some may have the opportunity to take early retirement or downsize to a part-time position. I know some employees would appreciate these sorts of solutions. So in the long run we're hoping we won't need to fire a hundred people.'

'So how many do you think?' asked Mia.

'It's impossible to say.'

'What about people who have short-term contracts, or those who have summertime jobs or are filling in for people on leave?' asked Forslund.

'We won't be hiring any new employees, and we're looking at reducing the sales staff,' said Pitkänen.

Now Erik was sitting in the car, going over the day in his mind as he drove. After the meeting everyone had been subdued, as if they'd received word of the death of someone they knew. They wouldn't find out how the restructuring would look until early July, in three weeks' time. He'd be out of the city when that happened.

He'd spoken to his immediate boss. Erik had noticed that Jouni wasn't particularly happy with his role. He seemed to think that life had unfairly placed him in this position, as a mid-level manager in an industry going through a crisis. It had always been evident to Erik that Jouni thought his future was abroad, or maybe as head of his own consulting firm.

'Too bad you're leaving on holiday right now. It would have been good if you could stay and participate in one of the groups,' said Jouni.

'I've been planning this summer holiday for several years. And I also have five weeks of overtime that I need to use,' said Erik.

'But the situation has changed. Surely you can see that.'

Erik shouldn't have been worried about his own job, but he was. He'd made a number of bad decisions lately and taken on projects that he could tell were not high on management's priority list.

'I don't know what to say. We're supposed to leave today,' said Erik.

'I don't know either. But, as we heard, we'll know more in July. I hope you enjoy your time in Ostrobothnia,' said Jouni.

Erik thought it was pointless to tell everyone about potential cutbacks in the middle of the summer holidays. Plenty of people were going to have a hard time enjoying their time off, but he realised – he'd read the newspapers – that this was happening in lots of Finnish workplaces at the moment. There was a general sense that everyone ought to grit their teeth in order to make it through these difficult times. No complaining allowed.

He could have sent Julia a text saying she should leave

without him, but when he was in the men's room on the second floor, where he'd retreated after lunch to read the job announcements on his mobile, he decided to take the tram home. He didn't want to disappoint Julia, and besides, she'd seemed a little distant lately. They'd hardly talked to each other over the past few months, and Erik worried that she might have grown tired of him. Julia was always so restless, always on her way somewhere. They needed a little time to themselves.

'How was work today?' asked Julia after they'd stopped to fill up the car at the petrol station just past Tammerfors. The nice weather had held, and Erik shifted down to pass a lorry.

'The usual. A holiday mood in the air. Lots of new summertime hires coming in. It's going to be great to get away from it all for a while.'

If he ended up unemployed this summer and couldn't find another job, they wouldn't be able to afford living in town much longer. Their living expenses were already too high. He decided not to say anything to Julia until he worked out what to do about the situation.

3

THEY ENCOUNTERED NO OTHER cars along the last few kilometres of the narrow forested road. They saw only a boy who looked to be about the same age as Alice. He was standing at the side of the road, holding a big stick and staring at their car as they drove past.

'Did you see that kid? There are other children here. That's great,' said Erik. He glanced in the rear-view mirror, thinking it was lucky he hadn't run over the boy, who had appeared out of nowhere.

'Maybe you'll make a new friend for the summer,' he added.

Alice had her headphones in and didn't hear a word.

They caught glimpses of the sea between the sparse pine trees. The water was smooth and grey, almost the same colour as the sky. It seemed to say: 'I have no intention of making a fuss just for your sake.' But it was still light outside, lighter than back in Helsinki, the sort of quiet and expansive midsummer light that lasts almost all day and night, and you don't really notice it until August when it vanishes as quickly as it arrived.

'The water looks cold,' said Anton.

'It'll be warmer in a few weeks,' said Julia.

Anton was the first one inside the summer house. He noticed

a raw, acrid smell when he crossed the threshold, but he didn't spend any time wondering where it came from. He was too busy wandering around and looking at everything, opening doors to all the rooms and cubbyholes, and feeling the solid wooden floorboards under his feet. In the main bedroom the walls were flecked with old damp spots, and the floor was littered with dust and dried pine needles. He opened one of the cubbyholes and found an old, yellowed dressing gown with a rip in one sleeve. He moved on to the living room and peered up at a brass clock decorated with writing in Finnish that he couldn't read. Above the big fireplace hung a wooden thermometer, and on the mantel was a heavy, old ashtray made of metal, in the shape of Finland.

Two whole months. That was an unimaginable length of time for Anton. When he thought about how it would seem when they came to the end of their holiday, he couldn't really picture it. The summer months quickly flickered past before his eyes. When the holiday was over, he would start in the fifth grade.

Now he went out on the terrace and showed his parents a little wooden house he'd found in the living room. He opened the roof.

'It's for cigarettes,' Julia told him. 'When you press on the chimney, a cigarette rolls out of the eaves. Like this. Watch.'

She pressed on the chimney.

'Could we buy some cigarettes?' asked Anton.

'Pappa and I don't smoke.'

'But Granny does. And she and Grandpa are coming here for Alice's birthday.'

'Granny smokes?'

'Sure. I saw her.'

'Maybe she used to smoke,' said Julia, glancing at Erik. 'Why don't you try putting something else inside. How about some sweets?'

'Okay. Good idea,' said Anton. And he went over to the car to fetch his bag of sweets.

Julia went inside the summer house. There was a double bed in the bedroom on the ground floor, with a narrow single bed against one wall. Both children would sleep in the attic. Up there the ceiling was low, and the air could be stifling because there were no openings for ventilation.

She went into the kitchen and opened the fridge, which was empty. It was from the seventies, dirty and a little rusty around the edges. The walls in the kitchen were covered with the same light-brown fabric wallpaper as the cupboards. The whole room was definitely in need of a good coat of paint or even a complete renovation, since the fabric seemed to have absorbed a lot of odours. There was pine everywhere. The chairs in the living room were made of lacquered pine, and the walls consisted of hewn logs that had also been lacquered. It must have been the height of modernity in its day. Julia's maternal grandmother had never had good taste. She had a fondness for slightly kitschy furnishings and little plaques with funny sayings. She was equally hopeless when it came to cooking, but she had compensated with other qualities. Julia would never forget how her grand-mother used to sit on the terrace in the evening, playing cards with her when everyone else had grown tired and gone to bed.

Erik walked around, inspecting the property. The morning meeting now seemed very distant, like an unsettling dream he had already shrugged off. He'd glanced at his mobile when they stopped in Jalasjärvi and noticed that he'd received more infor-mation from management, but he decided to put off reading it until Monday. He wanted to be alone, with no TV. He wanted to be a father again – something he'd hardly managed to do over the past few years. Now he planned to do everything fathers usually did: camping out, building a hut in the woods, cooking on the barbeque, maybe taking a boat out on the sea.

If his job could be said to have had a numbing effect on his emotional life, he would reclaim it through his family, especially out here in nature. He breathed in the fresh air as he looked at the clearly demarcated area of the property – this place where they were going to spend the next two months.

Julia's parents lived about ten kilometres from Mjölkviken. Erik knew it wouldn't be long before Julia's mother stood on the terrace, energetically waving her hands about and offering advice. Susanne possessed an unusual ability to know precisely what was best for everyone ('everyone except herself,' as Julia had said many times). Erik always tried to keep a certain distance from his mother-in-law. His own parents lived in Ekenäs. He hadn't spoken to them for some time now.

Erik's brother was in Vietnam on a 'find-yourself backpacking trip'. Anders was two years younger than Erik, but the age difference might as well have been ten years. Anders was someone who refused to grow up. He was always trying to re-invent himself by restlessly jumping from one thing to another.

Erik sat down at the small patio table on the mossy ground next to the little lake, called a tarn. Julia had told him that a few years back the whole tarn had been dredged so that the water was almost clear, but now it had silted up again and was filled with weeds and water lilies and algae. No one really knew how deep the water was, since the tarn had a soft, muddy bottom. Erik calculated it was at least fifty metres long and ten metres wide. In her first novel, Julia had described how a moose had swum across and then clambered ashore, nearly trampling a young child who was playing on the rocks outside the summer house.

Erik was sitting at a table that had been made from an old, gnarled pine tree. The chairs were made from the same tree, their legs twisted into odd shapes. The entire summer house was filled with these kinds of strange artefacts that had been acquired when the house was purchased.

He noticed now the sea breeze, even up here in the woods. He could hear the waves, a gentle and pleasant rushing sound that made him feel as if he were at the ends of the earth. When it got warmer, the air would smell of pine and salt water. In his mind Erik pictured the children, their downy suntanned backs covered with tiny grains of sand.

'Pappa, there's no coverage here. I can't even upload a picture.'

Alice was holding her mobile as she stood near the rocks below the house.

'Maybe it's better down at the beach,' he told her.

She cast a sceptical glance towards the shoreline.

'But maybe you won't need your phone now that we're here. There are plenty of things for us to do.'

'Like what?' she asked.

'I don't know. That's something you kids need to work out for yourselves. When I was a boy, we were always bored. It's good for kids to be bored.'

'So you're saying we came here to be bored?'

'I'm just saying that it's good for your sense of creativity if you're forced to think up things on your own. Look at your brother. He couldn't wait to get busy.'

Anton was sitting on the terrace, pressing on the chimney of the little wooden house he'd found.

Alice turned her sceptical gaze on her father.

'Excuse me if I'm not mentally backward like my brother. Even Spotify doesn't work out here.'

'There's a radio in the kitchen,' said Erik.

Alice groaned and headed inside the house.

Erik glanced down at his own mobile and read a headline from *Helsingin Sanomat*. A terrorist attack in Istanbul. Thirty-five people killed. He considered clicking on the link to read the article, but then he saw Julia come out onto the steps.

Should he mention it to her? Most likely she would read about it later, yet it could be that some sort of news threshold existed in a couple's relationship. Certain news was too big not to mention to your wife.

'There's been another terrorist attack. In Istanbul,' he called to her across the yard.

'Really?' she said. 'Is it bad?'

'I didn't read the article, but it says thirty-five people were killed.'

'That's awful,' said Julia, sitting down next to Anton on the terrace. 'Who did it?'

'I don't know. Probably ISIS.'

Anton looked up from the table, suddenly interested. He'd been asking a lot of questions about ISIS lately, wanting to talk about the situation in the world – wondering if there was any risk of terrorist attacks in Helsinki and whether Putin had plans to invade Finland.

'Pappa? You know what?' he said now.

Erik moved closer to the terrace.

'What?'

'I saw a film about somebody who made a list of the worst things you can do in a video game. There's a place in *Call of Duty 3* where you can be a terrorist and shoot down people in an airport.'

'That sounds horrible,' said Julia. 'Where did you see a film like that?'

'It was on YouTube. It wasn't so bad,' said Anton.

Erik glanced at Julia. They'd talked a lot about Anton's

fixation with YouTube, but had agreed that they needed to avoid the moralistic panic that had seized hold of their own parents when VHS players became popular back in the eighties.

Erik tried to open the link to the online article, but Alice was right, there was no coverage here. He walked around the yard for a while, going towards the woods behind the house, and finally managed to get a few bars on his mobile. It took for ever for the news site to open, but at last he saw a photograph. A bombed-out bus station, sagging steel beams, burned shops, shattered glass, crumpled road signs.

He read the article and then went back towards the house.

'The death toll is still rising,' he said as he went up the steps.

But Julia had already gone inside. Anton was still sitting on the terrace, all his attention focused on his new find. He'd managed to stick a few sweets inside the little house, and when he pressed on the chimney, a piece of liquorice tumbled out onto the eaves.

4

THE NEXT MORNING THEY were on their way down to the beach when they heard the sound of a tennis racket hitting a ball. There were several tennis courts nearby, a reminder of a time when Mjölkviken was new and modern, with families building stylish summer houses and buying motorised rubber boats. Erik pictured himself reserving time at a tennis court so he could learn to play the game properly. Maybe Julia would even be interested in joining him. She was so quick and agile.

'I think the sound is coming from over there,' said Alice with interest, pointing at a red-painted summer house nestled in a grove of pines close to the road. Erik caught a glimpse of the end of a net, but he couldn't see any players. They were walking along a path that led down to a small inlet with rounded slabs of reddish granite rocks and a big stretch of sandy beach.

Julia had told her family how much the area had changed over the past twenty years because the next generations seemed more and more obsessed with property lines.

'When I was a child, we were free to run everywhere. Nobody cared who happened to own the beach where we were playing. But these days none of the neighbours seem to spend much time with each other. Back then, this place was swarming with kids. I think people today lead such comfortable lives that they don't feel like going out to the seashore any more. It's too quiet and too far from all the conveniences of the city,' she explained.

Anton looked at his mother, trying to imagine how it must have been when there were other children here. At the same time, he thought it was nice that his family had the place all to themselves. It always took such an effort to get to know new people.

'Maybe we just need to talk to our neighbours. That shouldn't be so hard, should it?' said Erik.

Julia looked at him.

'You can try. I think most of them are retired couples. Families with young kids don't come here any more,' she told him.

When they reached the shore, she sat down on the sand and poured herself a cup of coffee from the thermos.

The water was cold, and Anton didn't want to swim, even though his father tried to persuade him.

'It'll be warmer in a few weeks,' said Erik. 'It's not even midsummer yet. But the air is warm. Have you noticed? If you can find a sheltered place to lie down, that is,' he added, turning his face to see which direction the wind was coming from. But it was hard to find a place to sit. The rocks were too low-lying to offer much protection from the wind. He sat down and leaned against a rock that felt much colder than he'd expected. It was as if winter were still lingering in the ground, as if it hadn't yet relinquished its grip entirely.

Julia didn't seem bothered by the wind. She sat in the pale sunlight, her eyes closed.

'It's so beautiful here,' said Erik emphatically, loud enough that the others would hear. If he scrunched down slightly, he couldn't feel the wind.

Julia merely looked at him for a moment and then went back to sunbathing.

The children lay on their towels as they listened to the ricocheting tennis ball.

'It must be the rocks that make it echo like that, as if the sound is coming from the sea,' said Erik.

'Kind of depressing to play tennis all by yourself,' said Alice. Julia looked up.

'An old couple used to live there. It must be their son who's playing. I suppose he still comes out here once in a while.'

'I'm freezing,' said Anton.

'Stop whining,' said Alice, prompting Anton to give her a swift kick.

'Here, wrap up in a towel,' said Erik. 'And come closer to me. It's not so windy over here next to the rocks.'

Julia poured herself a third cup of coffee. She was planning to start on her next book this summer, and now here she sat in the sun, thinking about it and refusing to let the family distract her.

That was the reason she had agreed to come here. Two months of isolation from the rest of the world was exactly what she needed to get going. She was going to write a novel about women in Jakobstad in the mid-twentieth century, and about the old tobacco factory which, at the time, was the town's biggest employer. That was where her maternal grandmother had worked. Julia already had in mind the main character – a young woman who got a job there in the forties and then ended up pregnant by one of the factory managers. In Julia's mind, the novel was practically written already. She had interviewed former workers at the factory – she'd been awarded a grant for that purpose – and she had looked at thousands of photographs from back then. She had also visited the local museum, with its collection of items from the factory: old drawings for cigarette packs, labels, time cards and adverts.

She was going to sit in the kitchen and write. This morning she'd looked through her notes and decided she needed an overall theme on which to base her story. Something a little more compelling. She thought about the post-war era with all the torn-apart families, all the alcoholic men who came home from the frontlines, all the young women who were forced to care for their brothers and fathers.

That had led to a few pages, and she wanted to continue with her writing after lunch. She was quite pleased with what she'd written so far. But it was always like that. The beginning was not the hard part.

When she looked up, she realised how much this place had affected her, with all the colours and rocks, the scent of the pine forest and the damp, marshy ground. It was all so familiar from her childhood. They were sitting across from one of the big rocks where she and Marika used to sunbathe. They would spread their towels out on the hot smooth surface and lie there talking. One summer the rocks had been covered with ladybirds, which had kept them preoccupied for a long while. Yet there was something not quite right about that memory; something was giving her goose pimples. It had always felt a little strange to leave the city behind and come out here, where the grown-ups behaved as if all the family boundaries had somehow dissolved. She had written a novel about Mjölkviken and left her childhood behind.

'I think I'll go back now,' she said, brushing off the sand. 'I want to try to do a little writing before lunch.'

'Sure, go ahead. The kids and I will stay here for a while. Okay?' said Erik. 'Shall we make a sand castle?'

'Yes!' said Anton, dropping his towel next to Erik.

The children began building a sand castle at the water's edge while Julia packed up her things. Erik gave her a look meant to encourage her. His eager support made her feel stressed, as if she were indebted to him because he was so understanding, as if she ought to finish writing the first chapter of her novel before lunch.

She picked up the thermos and her beach blanket and walked back up to the house. She caught a glimpse of the tennis court, but hurried past. She wasn't ready to socialise with the local populace just yet.

When the sand castle was finished, Alice walked along the shore and went out to the furthest promontory of rocks. There she looked out at the sea. She wished the waves were bigger and a real storm was raging. That would have been more fun to photograph. Maybe there would be storms later in the summer. She thought about her classmates and was glad to be out here right now. Several of the kids she knew were going to spend the summer abroad: taking a road trip through Italy or visiting New York. Her mother was a writer, and Alice had learned that meant they didn't have as much money as her classmates.

Erik and Anton had begun skimming stones across the water. Alice resumed walking among the rocks. The heather caressed her legs as she climbed from one rock to another. She noticed there was better coverage out here, so she took a picture of the sea and uploaded it to Instagram: '#vacation #summer #boring #sea #helpme'.

She continued clambering further along the bay, jumping from a rock into the cold water, choosing a cleft so Anton and Erik wouldn't see her.

The water was shallow, barely reaching to her knees, and clear. The sand under her feet felt pleasant and cold, as if she were walking on a very soft rug. She walked further and further away from Anton and her father.

Alice had started having her periods this spring. It was as if she'd suddenly grown up on that first day, as if everything in the world had abruptly changed and she could no longer view things with the same childish eyes. Her mother and father seemed different. Everyone in school seemed different, more ridiculous somehow. Above all, she herself felt different. Not in a bad way, but she found it hard to say whether it was better or not. She could hardly remember how she'd felt before. The summer holiday was a welcome break from everything. She hated wearing a swimsuit, but it was tolerable with only her family to see her. They didn't stare at all the awkward angles of her body, at the bony crook of her arm, or at her podgy feet.

Her mother had told her not to obsess about her body, that all those expectations came from external sources, or 'social constructs', as she called them. But Alice wondered whether it was really that simple. When she looked at herself in the mirror, it didn't seem like she was looking through someone else's eyes; she was the one who was dissatisfied. She was too short and her nose looked wrong in profile, as if somebody had pressed it slightly towards her face. She'd heard that she had her father's nose, but she didn't think it suited her.

A house stood on the shore across the bay. It was painted grey and looked quite modern, as if it were no more than ten years old. It seemed to be vacant. Alice was on her way towards this house when she caught sight of something gleaming in the water. She nudged it with her toe, then tried to pick it up with her foot. When she poked at it again, it floated to the surface. A ring. She plucked it from the water and studied it. The ring was smooth and not especially big. A woman's ring. And Alice saw a date etched on the inside. Through the drops of water she read: *19.4.1994.*

She glanced behind her. Her father and Anton were still playing that ridiculous game of skimming stones. She wanted to tell them about the ring, and yet she wanted to keep it to herself. She thought it might make the discovery seem more important if she told them, but they might react in the wrong way. Even worse would be if they didn't react at all, but merely shrugged.

She considered taking a picture of the ring but that didn't seem right. The ring was hers.

She stood there in the cold water for a moment, contemplating what to do. In the end, she decided not to tell anyone.

By the time Alice got back to the beach, Anton had already gone up to the house.

'Isn't it great out here?' said her father.

'Sure,' said Alice.

The sun had broken through the clouds, and it was now warm enough to lie down and dry off. Alice spent the rest of the morning like that, wrapped in a gentle indolence. The milk-white sky was as motionless as her thoughts, with only the quiet gurgling of the water audible from somewhere in the background, interrupted now and then by the tennis-playing sounds of the neighbour. Alice slipped in and out of sleep. In her hand she held the ring, which she planned to study more closely later.

5

FREEZING COLD, HIS LIPS blue, Anton walked up towards the house without the others.

'Mamma, do you think there are snakes here?' he asked as Julia brushed the sand off his legs and handed him his clothes.

'I'm sure there are. But I've only ever seen one.'

'When was that?'

'Back when I was a little girl and your great-grandfather was still alive. It was behind the sauna. But that was a long time ago.'

'Was it a viper?'

'I think so.'

'What did you do with it?'

'I think your grandfather hit it with a shovel and sliced it in two.'

Julia actually had a vivid memory of the event. Her family was having a party, and the grown-ups were all drunk. She must have been seven or eight, and some of the guests had seen a snake behind the house when they went there to take a piss. Everybody went over to have a look. It was a very big viper, lying motionless on a bare patch of ground behind the sauna. Julia was shocked when her father fetched a shovel and abruptly chopped the snake in half while everyone else cheered. Somebody stepped forward and poured beer over the snake. She hadn't been prepared to witness her father killing a snake. The sudden violence made her blood turn cold.

'But that's the only time I've ever seen a snake out here, so I don't think there are many of them. Although I suppose it would be wise to be cautious,' she said now.

Anton seemed to be thinking about what she'd just said. He looked around the yard, as if picturing snakes everywhere.

'Mamma,' he said.

'Yes?'

'Do you remember Valter, who went to my pre-school? A snake bit him, and he was almost paralysed.'

'I know. His mother told me about it.'

The boy had suffered a bad snake bite at a summer house somewhere out in the Åboland archipelago. He had to be airlifted by helicopter to a hospital, and he was forced to spend several weeks in a wheelchair. The teachers at the pre-school had told the other children how to protect themselves from snake bites.

'If you're worried about it, you can always wear your rubber boots when you're outside. And it might be best if you wear them when you run around in the woods,' said Julia.

'Okay. I will,' said Anton.

A short time later Erik and Alice came back from the beach.

'I've been thinking about that man playing tennis,' said Erik. 'I think I'll ask if I can play a game with him someday. I might be good at it. Would you like to play too?'

'I think his name is Leif. His mother was friends with my grandmother,' said Julia.

Erik went into the kitchen and poured each of them a glass of water. Then he sat at the table, silently staring out of the window.

'You'll probably get a lot written this summer, I suppose?' he said. It sounded more like a statement than a question.

Julia was twenty-three when she and Erik got married. She used to say that it was her mother Susanne who proposed to Erik.

That it was Susanne who suggested having a wedding since they were expecting a child.

'Of course you have to get married,' Susanne said one evening during the Christmas holidays, speaking with all the authority of a grown-up, as if Julia and Erik were still too young to make any decisions on their own.

And maybe that was true. When Julia stood in the Old Church of Helsinki a few months later, listening to the pastor, who insisted on calling Erik 'Henrik', she still wasn't sure what exactly was happening.

Her wedding gown was made of cream-coloured silk. She'd bought it for only five euros at the UFF second-hand shop on Stora Robertsgatan on the day when she and Erik went to the doctor and saw the first ultrasound images. The dress draped beautifully over her stomach, which she imagined had already begun to show her pregnancy. She was happy and in love, though a little shocked by how fast everything had proceeded.

Afterwards at the restaurant, everyone drank too much. Susanne finished off a whole bottle of white wine, which the waitress had set at their end of the table, and then followed with a glass of cognac as she talked boisterously. Julia could hear that her mother was telling someone about her dress, which she'd bought from the same designer who made many of the evening gowns worn at the president's independence day ball at the palace. Susanne remarked that she knew the designer person- ally, so she'd got the dress for a good price.

'He said he'd actually designed it with me in mind,' Susanne added as she drained her cognac glass. 'Normally it would have cost a fortune, but I think he likes to have high-profile customers ...'

Erik's mother merely nodded politely, peering attentively at all the guests without saying much. Susanne kept on talking, though occasionally she would pause briefly to survey the others seated at the table, her expression a bit disapproving, as if she now realised that her daughter had married into a 'sausage family'. That was what she called people she considered to be low-brow or ordinary.

Erik's family was a sausage family. His parents had arrived the day before by train from Ekenäs and had eaten dinner in the hotel restaurant. They had studied the menu for what seemed like an eternity and then ordered the simplest dish on offer: steak and chips.

Erik's father had left school at the age of fifteen back in the sixties, and after that he went to work for a company in Hangö that changed tyres. He worked in the automotive industry for fifteen years, married Erik's mother – who had grown up in the same neighbourhood – and eventually became the proprietor of his own petrol station in Ekenäs. At the wedding supper, he drank almost as much as Susanne, talking mostly about a flat the family had owned in Spain back in the eighties – clearly an attempt on his part to raise, at least partially, the social stakes at the table. For Erik and his brother Anders, their working-class background was a constant source of pride, and Julia had even felt a bit jealous of them – the fact that they had deliberately risen in social class while she had merely done what everyone had always expected of her. She was capable and diligent and had chosen the natural path for any self-respecting member of the eighties generation with well-to-do academic parents: a highly uncertain career within the cultural sphere.

Julia met Erik for the first time at the Old Student House, or student union, at a party organised by the student association of the literature institute. Erik was studying IT and lived in student housing in Otnäs. Julia had taken pity on him when he missed the last bus home. After that night, they spent nearly every day together for the next five weeks, although nothing happened between them. They even talked about the fact that they had such a good relationship because it was not based on sex. At that time Julia had a boyfriend, but it wasn't serious enough for her to hesitate about inviting Erik to spend the night. She had actually been waiting for an opportunity to break off the relationship. Tomas was an assistant librarian at the literature institute and nearly ten years older, although he didn't act like it. He was clumsy in bed and had bad breath. The only reason Julia hadn't broken up with him before was because he seemed to be someone who had suffered rejection too many times in his life.

Erik and Julia began going to the theatre and the cinema together, yet they were both so busy thinking about each other that afterwards neither of them could ever remember what the play or film was about.

One night they ended up sitting on a park bench somewhere in Havshagen after taking a long walk, and they started talking, hypothetically, about becoming a couple. The air seemed to pulse with tension, and they were both shivering with cold as they stared at a man who was fishing out on the ice.

Erik and Julia had constructed a story in which they were merely friends, but Julia could feel how she tingled with desire whenever she looked at him. Erik was twenty-one and planning to enter the mobile phone business when he finished his studies. He seemed filled with self-confidence and faith in the future.

'What do you think about becoming a couple? How would that work?' she asked, looking at him.

'It would be awful,' he said, and then smiled. It was so cold outside that vapour issued from his mouth. He was very handsome, though he seemed unaware of that fact – which only increased his charm.

'Horrible,' she said, and laughed.

'You'd soon get sick and tired of me. You'd think I was boring, with lots of boring friends,' he said.

'You'd study all day long, and I'd be home trying to write my masterpiece.'

Julia had decided to become a writer. She'd told Erik about this, with some embarrassment, because she thought it sounded a little pretentious, but he had reacted in exactly the right way. He had encouraged her and said she should set aside at least two hours a day for her writing. He had taken a completely practical view, considering it a goal worth pursuing, almost in the same way as if she'd wanted to be a doctor. She admired his pragmatic attitude. She wasn't used to that back home, where everyone expected that she would succeed as if by magic.

'And then I'd come home and you'd be cross because you didn't get any writing done,' he said.

'And finally I'd get so frustrated because of writer's block that I'd start talking to myself, and then I'd find an axe and start chasing you around the flat like Jack Nicholson in *The Shining*,' said Julia.

'Great film,' said Erik.

'Hmm … I was only fourteen when I read the book. That's always what I think about when I don't get any writing done. All work and no play makes Jack a dull boy.'

'But there would be one positive note: I'd cook great food. You'd eat well,' said Erik.

Julia laughed.

'Wonderful. I hate to cook.'

'So maybe it would work out after all.'

'Maybe it would.'

Now, as he sat here in the kitchen and asked Julia whether she was hungry and whether he should light the barbecue, it felt as if those two people existed only in old photo albums. And Julia felt both touched and embarrassed when she thought about how young they had been.

Julia admired Erik and knew that he was a good father, but sometimes she felt quite lonely when she was with him. She would look at other couples and think that they didn't seem to be experiencing the same sort of loneliness. Other couples seemed to belong together, and they were so obviously fond of each other. She felt guilty that she didn't feel the same way about Erik, which made her even lonelier, since there was no one she could talk to about this. She considered it to be the greatest possible betrayal, this yearning to get away. And she wasn't even certain that's what it was. Maybe her loneliness stemmed from something else, something existentially indefinable – the incurable ennui of modern times. She often thought about *Madame Bovary*, which she'd read during her first year at university. Maybe she was no better than Emma Bovary – equally naïve in her longing, equally enticed by some sort of imagined adventure that might break up the monotony of everyday life. But Emma Bovary was barely an adult, while Julia would soon turn thirty-six. Wasn't she too old to be yearning to get away? Shouldn't she have grown out of that phase of her life?

'Do you know when your parents will arrive?' asked Erik.

'Probably in a couple of days,' she said.

'Are they going to sleep here?'

'I doubt it. I don't think they've slept here in ages. Besides, there's no room for them.'

'They could sleep up in the attic.'

'It's too hot in the attic for Mamma. She's always complaining about it. They'll probably drive back home.'

'Or else they'll stay here, and she'll walk around the whole time in her underwear, like in Spain,' said Erik.

'I forgot about that,' said Julia, now recalling the trip they'd taken to Spain two years ago. Susanne had slept every night on the sofa, clad in her underwear, worn out and numbed by the wine she'd had from the wine-in-a-box she'd bought at the local shop.

It had felt like spending the holidays with a force of nature, a storm with a will of its own. Susanne was the sort of person who might ask the children what they wanted to do in the morning, and then forget all about their wishes and spend the day following her own plans. For Susanne, being able to talk about how she'd spent the holiday with her grandchildren was more important than actually doing anything with them.

'Well, it'll be fun to see them, no matter what,' said Erik.

'Really?' said Julia.

'At least for the kids. And your mother means well. She can be a little much sometimes, but she's basically good-hearted.'

'I suppose so. At any rate, I don't think they'll stay long,' said Julia.

The wind picked up in the evening. Erik cooked dinner on the barbecue, but they ate inside because it was too cold to sit outdoors. As Julia rinsed off her plate after dinner, she noticed a strange smell. She pressed her nose against the fabric covering the walls, but it smelled only of old sackcloth.

'Do you notice that?' she asked.

'What?' asked Erik.

'There's an odd smell,' said Julia.

'All old houses smell odd,' he replied.

'You don't think we have a mould problem?' she said.

'That doesn't seem likely. Where would it be?'

'I don't know, but I think it smells damp. But maybe I'm just imagining things.'

'When it gets warmer, we can air the place out,' said Erik. 'And then you can sit outside to write instead of in the kitchen. But I'll check it out. Maybe there's something your father and I can do about it when they get here.'

After dinner the kids retreated to the living room where they tried to get the old television to work. Julia and Erik stayed sitting at the kitchen table. Julia thought she should spend every day writing, and she wondered whether she would do just that – isolating herself completely for the rest of the summer and letting Erik take care of everything else.

Erik was holding his mobile, staring at it.

'What's wrong?' she asked.

'Nothing,' he said, sticking the phone in his pocket. 'I just wanted to see if we had any coverage here.'

Erik took his mobile to the beach so he could check his emails in peace.

The bay was deserted. He saw only the heavy, restless clouds that shrank the landscape. A strong wind was creating big waves further out. After a while he started to freeze.

He stared at his phone. For a moment he considered flinging it into the sea so no one could reach him. Instead, he called the number that had been trying to reach him all day. It was a number he knew well.

'Hi! How's it going?' asked Jouni. He was clearly at work because Erik could hear sounds coming from the department store in the background.

'Good, thanks. Everything's great,' he replied.

They spoke for two minutes and forty seconds. He made note of the time on the display afterwards as he stared at the phone and wondered what he should do. It was true that they'd promised him severance pay. Six months' salary, which wasn't bad. The last thing Jouni said was: 'I'm sorry, Erik. I'm really sorry.'

When Erik stepped through the door, the kids had just brought their bedclothes downstairs so they could sleep in their parents' bedroom. Anton said he was afraid of snakes, and Alice refused to sleep up in the attic alone because she thought it was horrible.

'You'll have to sleep head to toe in that little bed,' said Julia.

It was still light outside, a muted, grey light, and Julia hung a blanket over the window to make the room dark. Anton wanted to know whether there were tadpoles in the woods.

'I'm sure there are,' said Julia. 'At least, there used to be when I was a little girl. Goodnight, you two.'

Later, after they'd turned off the lights and the kids were asleep, Erik lay in bed wide awake for a long time.

'Are you asleep?' he finally asked.

'No, not yet,' said Julia.

'Feel like having sex?'

'Now? Here?'

'I was thinking up in the attic. So we don't wake the kids.'

They tiptoed up the stairs, which creaked under their feet. There were two big rooms, one on either side of the stairs. Both were dark because the ceilings were low and the windows small. In one room was a double bed, and they lay down on it. The whole time Erik had a feeling that Julia was responding stronger than usual, as if her body were more sensitive to his touch here, and he wondered whether it was because of this place, in this dark and stifling room with the woods outside the window and the current low pressure – as if she were a barometer. It was a similar experience for Erik. With every touch, during every second of sex, he felt fully present, and yet it seemed like a film, as if he were looking at both of them from the outside. She climbed on top of him and he looked up. He saw Julia's dark hair, her soft breasts, and the beams in the ceiling. He happened to think that it had probably been a long time since anyone had had sex in this room. Maybe it had never happened before. At the same time, as he felt himself on the verge of coming, he also thought about his job and the phone conversation with Jouni, about Riina Pitkänen and the way she'd stood in front of the room during the meeting. Suddenly he pictured her naked, holding a whip in her hand, wearing stiletto heels, and bending over the conference table.

Afterwards they went back downstairs. He felt strangely happy and warm. They walked through the silent house in the muted summer light to get a glass of water in the kitchen. He thought that life was quite wonderful, even though maybe he should have felt differently now that he'd lost his job.

'That was intense,' said Julia.

'It sure was,' said Erik.

They lay awake in bed for a while, without talking. When Julia finally fell asleep, Erik thought he could hear a tennis ball striking a backboard outside. He couldn't believe anyone would be playing tennis at this time of night. And even if they were, could it really be heard up here?

6

'WAIT FOR ME,' SAID Anton. He always had the feeling that Alice knew so much more than he did, which gave her an advantage. She was only three years older, and that worried Anton. Would he be able to learn everything in three years? It was a mystery how people managed to learn things at all. He'd noticed it did no good to ask his parents. They were so busy with their own interests. Instead, he learned most things from YouTube, clicking from one video to another to find out about everything from computer games and basketball shoes to American politics.

Anton could never get a straight answer from his father, only a vague hemming and hawing. His question would get swallowed up in a feeling that there were lots of different ways to look at matters. Anton didn't understand how that could be true. Either there were snakes or there weren't. That should be simple enough to work out.

Right now Alice was walking ahead of him along the road. It was Sunday, and they'd left as soon as breakfast was finished to see if they could find any tadpoles. It was sixteen degrees Celsius, warm enough to wear a T-shirt. Anton had never seen a tadpole, so he didn't quite know what to expect. Would he be able to hold one? His mother had said they were so fast that it would be hard to catch them. Down at the beach this morning, his father had Googled tadpoles and found out this was a good time to catch them because the eggs had been laid back in April.

'Although I'm not really sure … it says here that they hatch in April to May. You'll just have to go and scope out the real situation,' he added, causing Anton to sigh.

They had turned off onto a narrow path. Anton followed Alice, carrying a bucket in one hand and keeping his eyes on the ground in front of him.

'We should have brought a cup to catch them with,' said Alice. 'That bucket is too big. We'll come back again if we find any.'

'Do you think there are any snakes out here?' he asked.

He was wearing his rubber boots. They were black and felt hot because he'd put them on over his bare feet. He peered down at the blueberry bushes along the edge of the ditch, imagining how a snake might jump out and bite him. He hadn't yet decided whether he liked nature or not. In many ways it seemed dangerous and troublesome, and he missed the shops and the security of Helsinki. Since his father worked at the department store in the centre of town, he'd always had access to that world. He'd been allowed to see everything in the warehouse that none of the customers ever saw, and he'd sat in the staff room to drink juice. He liked going to work with his father. The women who worked there all smelled so good, and there were so many of them that someone always paid special attention to him. He liked the atmosphere in the electronics department. Everything looked as if it had just been taken out of the packaging, all shiny and new. It seemed like an amazing place to work because all his father had to do was repair some internet connections once in a while. Often it only required turning off the internet and then switching it back on.

'Over there,' Alice said now.

She pointed at a big pool of water that had formed on the ground in a glade in the woods. Nearby stood an old trailer, grey and mossy, covered with a green tarp.

They went over to the pool and looked closer. The murky water was filled with leaves. Alice leaned down and touched the water.

'It's warm,' she said. 'Find me a stick.'

Anton looked around. Everywhere he saw blueberries and lingonberries growing. The trunks of the slender pine trees shifted from grey to reddish-brown where animals had gnawed away the bark. He picked up a branch from the ground, broke off two twigs, and handed them to Alice.

They leaned over the water, surrounded by the smell of old leaves. The bottom of the pool was black, and Anton could see his own face mirrored in the water. His blond hair looked darker than usual. He looked like his mother. When Alice used the stick to stir the water, the leaves whirled up and shredded.

'I don't see anything. This is boring,' she said, disappointed. She kept swatting mosquitoes away from her forehead as she stuck her foot in the water.

'I don't understand why they sent us out here to walk around in the woods. There's nothing but a bunch of mosquitoes.'

'Maybe they're hiding under the leaves,' said Anton, feeling a certain tenderness at the thought of the tadpoles swimming away. Occasionally he had this sort of feeling, though he didn't know why. It was almost enough to make him cry, so he'd try to think of something else. Often he'd think about his classmate Amin, who liked to wear a wrestling mask in gym class. Amin was a serious boy, just like Anton, and they spent a lot of time together, even though they hadn't really established that they were best friends. Anton would also think about Oona, and how soft she was when she hugged him, and how nice she was when they played Monopoly. She was stern yet nice.

He stepped into the water, wearing his rubber boots and dragging his stick along the bottom. At first he didn't see anything, but out of the corner of his eye he noticed a swift movement.

'There!'

When he leaned closer, he saw tiny black tadpoles. There were a lot of them, and they swam away when he moved his stick towards them.

'We need something smaller to catch them. Go back to the house and fetch a cup,' said Alice.

'No. I don't want to,' said Anton, looking up from the pool. He had no desire to walk back alone.

'But there's nothing to be scared of,' said Alice. 'You can run the whole way. I want to take some nature photographs, and we'll be able to see the tadpoles better in a cup.'

He'd been nervous enough walking back from the beach alone yesterday, and that wasn't as far. The whole time he'd told himself that he'd be seeing his mother very soon, and that had helped.

'No. You go. I'm the one who found them,' he said now.

Anton felt a wild fury surging inside him, as often happened. It was a sense of injustice that came from his gut and made him want to shove his sister.

'So you're too scared?' she said. 'If we're going to be here all summer, you'll have to learn to walk around alone. You can't be hanging on to me all the time.'

In the end Anton agreed to go. The whole time he had a feeling that he was being watched, that someone was following him. He paused about halfway and thought he heard someone stepping on a twig in the woods, but when he listened closely, he heard only a rushing sound from the sea.

Then he picked up his pace, almost running, with a feeling that fear must be visible on the outside of his body, that anyone who looked at him would see it.

When he got close to the house he met his parents, who were on their way down to the bay. Julia was carrying two tennis rackets.

'Mamma, I found some tadpoles,' he called.

'Can I see?' she said.

'They're in the woods.'

'Where's Alice?'

'She's waiting for me. I have to fetch a cup.'

'Okay. Then come down to the tennis court later. We're going to play a game.'

'Can't you come with me?' asked Anton.

'No. You can go up to the house yourself. There are plastic cups in the kitchen cupboard. On the left when you go into the kitchen.'

'But it's creepy in there. I don't want to go alone.'

'What do you mean, it's creepy? I stayed here for weeks at a time when I was a kid. It's just an ordinary kitchen.'

Anton thought about Alice in the woods and the fact that he needed to fetch a cup and then head back the same way he'd come. He had to go back and find her in the glade.

He gathered his courage and walked up the path towards the house. After opening the door he stepped inside cautiously, as if trying to avoid frightening any potential intruders when he went into the kitchen. He quickly found the cups and didn't waste time looking around. He focused all his attention on the task at hand and then dashed out of the house.

As he headed for the road he thought about Amin again, and how hard it was to know whether they were best friends or not, because it wasn't something they ever talked about. The afternoons simply slipped by without them making any decisions. In fact, maybe it was Iiris who was his best friend. She lived across the street and was in his class, but they never spent time together in school. Instead, they saw each other in the evening, or whenever their parents invited each other over for dinner. He felt closer to Iiris than to anyone else. Only a few days ago they had been sitting in his room, both of them with a solemn feeling because he was going to be gone all summer. They'd talked about how practical it would be if he had his own helicopter. Then he could fly back and forth and land on the roof in Tölö if they were going to meet. He'd wondered if he might be in love with Iiris, but something told him that was a different sort of feeling.

One time he'd gone to his room to cry because he could hear in her voice that she didn't want to play with him. He'd cried for a while, until finally he found himself thinking more about the fact that he was crying than about Iiris, because disappointment was something new for him. That night his mother had come into his room, as if she knew what was going on, and they'd sat there together, under the posters on his wall, and he'd thought it had been one of the best days ever because he'd been able to feel so much.

Alice was gone when he returned to the glade in the woods. He made a few attempts to find her, walking around the pool of water where he'd left her, but after a while he felt a growing uneasiness and decided to leave. He walked purposefully back, quickly passing the empty summer houses along the road and heading for the bay to find his parents.

When he reached the tennis court, there was Alice sitting on the grass.

'Where did you go? I went all the way back there for nothing,' he said.

Alice had her headphones in and merely stared at him.

Anton was out of breath after walking so far, but he forgot all about that when he heard a low rumble coming from the other side of the bay. It sounded like muted trumpet blasts at ten-second intervals. Alice didn't react. Anton looked up at the tops of the pine trees in the direction of the sound.

His parents also stopped playing to listen to the rumbling.

'That's odd,' said Erik.

'Maybe it's a boat horn?' suggested Julia.

'It sounded closer than that,' said Anton.

After a while the sound stopped. Then all they could hear was a flock of seagulls somewhere near the shore, shrieking and screeching, as if they'd found an easy catch.

His parents kept playing tennis all morning. Anton played with his mother for a while but tired of the game. Then he bounced a ball off his racket into the air. He managed to bounce the ball nearly fifty times before dropping it.

The grown-ups were good at playing tennis. Julia hit ball after ball and ran around the cracked asphalt like a nimble deer.

Anton sat on the grass, watching her. He saw how light on her feet she was, and he noticed the way she pushed her hair back when it fell over her forehead. Clearly tennis was one of the things a person could learn somewhere, because he hadn't known that his mother could play. His father moved more stiffly, and he had an annoyed expression on his face, even though he was trying hard to look happy. It was like when Anton visited his paternal grandmother and they were given some strange-looking food with a bunch of weird vegetables and he tried to be polite. That's how his father looked right now, maybe because he was losing.

'Shit,' his father called from the court. 'I need better shoes.'

When his parents finished their game, they sat down on the grass and drank some water from the bottles they'd brought along. They were just about to head back to the summer house when a man came walking over to the tennis court from the beach. He had close-cropped hair, a flat stomach and a smile that seemed suntanned.

'Hi,' he said. 'Do you speak English?'

Julia nodded. 'Of course.'

'That's great. We're staying down there near the beach,' the man said, pointing towards the bay. 'We've been here a few weeks now. I apologise for the noise. We're making preparations. I thought I'd come over and invite you to the party on Midsummer Eve. There'll be food and wine, a bonfire and maybe some politics, if you can stand that sort of discussion.'

'That sounds interesting,' said Erik.

'Uh-huh. It usually is. I'm Chris, by the way,' he said, shaking hands with all of them, including Alice and Anton. He had a firm handshake. He smiled again and remarked on how wonderful the weather was, although the weather wasn't especially wonderful.

'Well, anyway,' he said. 'You're welcome to join us next Friday.'

'Thanks. We'll give it some thought,' said Erik.

The man looked at Julia, who nodded and tucked a sweaty strand of hair behind her ear.

part two

the others

1

JULIA WALKED ALONG, carrying two bottles of wine in a sack. The heels of her shoes sank into the soft sand. It was five o'clock on Midsummer Eve, and the weather was now a little warmer. A fleeting warmth interspersed with cool breezes from the sea. They had driven into town earlier in the day to shop for groceries.

'We won't stay long,' she said. 'I want to write in the morning.'

'You can't work all the time. Let's just see how the evening goes, okay?' said Erik.

He'd dressed up for the occasion. A sport coat, jeans, black socks, black shoes. Julia hadn't said anything to him, although she had the impression these were not the sort of people they needed to dress up for. The man they'd met was older than Julia and Erik, but he had that type of carefree air about him that could be found among physically fit men of a certain age.

She wished she'd worn sandals instead of heels.

'We don't need to both leave at the same time,' she said. She was thinking how nice it would be to go home earlier and sit on the terrace or in the kitchen, and have a glass of wine all alone.

'How long do you think we should leave the kids on their own?' asked Erik.

'They have their phones. They can always ring us if something comes up. And they can come over to fetch us if they want.'

'Maybe there will be other children,' he said, as he turned on his mobile.

Julia had noticed that Erik had been looking at his phone more often the past few days, as if he couldn't quite tear himself away from his job. She'd told him it was okay if he wanted to answer any emails. Maybe he should spend a few hours each day working, if he needed to. But then he got defensive and muttered that he was on holiday and was just checking Facebook. Maybe she should have been suspicious and wondered if he had another woman, but Erik wasn't like that. He was too distracted, maybe even too childish.

Julia felt depressed at the thought of having to meet new people right now, just as she sometimes felt depressed before a publishing party in the city. Social events always required effort. Yet she was a little curious about the man who had introduced himself to them. She wondered what these people were like, especially since they seemed to be staying in the Segerkvists' old house, where her friend Marika had lived. Erik might be right, maybe a break was exactly what she needed after writing for a whole week.

'Do you think they invited other neighbours?' asked Erik.

'What other neighbours?'

'Surely there must be other people around here. I can't believe all the houses are empty,' he said. 'What about that man, for instance? The one who plays tennis?'

'Who knows,' said Julia.

'He mentioned they were serving food, right? I'm starving,' said Erik.

The house was one of the most beautiful on the shore. Julia had been there often as a child. Marika's father was a paediatrician in the city. Marika was a year older than Julia, and she talked like a grown-up, as if she was trying to imitate her parents. She had thick, curly hair. That was what Julia remembered most about her, how her hair had looked when they went swimming or lay on the floor inside the house and played. Everything was always on Marika's terms, because she had taken on all her parents' attitudes and opinions about how the world should be organised. In Julia's first novel, she had given Marika a different name, but many of the scenes were taken directly from her own memories, which often were about following around after Marika and doing what she wanted. Julia hadn't personally analysed what she'd written, but when the book was published, several critics said the novel dealt with the sort of co-dependence that was typical for young girls. Julia had never dared oppose Marika. She'd spent all her free time with her, even though there were occasions when she didn't really want to. She'd often had a feeling that she would have preferred to be alone. But then she would have had to explain to Marika what she'd been doing instead, and that would have given rise to lies that would lead to more lies, which would make Julia feel so guilty that she thought it was simpler to play with Marika. And they often did have fun, although Marika was given to strange outbursts of anger and jealousy, and then Julia had to suffer the brunt of her moods. One critic had described her novel as an allegory for the relationships that many women have with men who are no good.

The house was a low, one-storey building, painted brown, with big windows facing the beach. Elegant sixties-style architecture, nothing lavish, but Julia had always liked this type of house.

The new owners had put up a yurt in a clearing closer to the woods. It looked monstrous and yet childish next to the summery functionalism of the house. It was rather like an oversize Indian tepee.

A man in his thirties with dreadlocks and dressed in baggy shorts was walking around the yard talking on his mobile on speaker. A younger dark-haired woman stood in the sand, using a towel to dry herself off.

Julia and Erik were greeted by an older couple who emerged naked from a sauna and waved hello. Julia tried not to look at Erik because she knew if she did she would start laughing.

'Nice to meet you,' said the woman.

'Julia,' said Julia, stepping forward.

'Ylva. And this is Roger,' said the woman, giving him a light pat on the arse.

They shook hands. Ylva had long grey hair that lay in wet coils over her breasts. She was suntanned and plump and looked to be between sixty-five and seventy.

'Are you the ones who have rented the summer house?' asked Julia.

'No, of course not. This is Marika and Chris's place. They live here. Roger and I are just guests. We're from Borgå.'

Julia felt the hair on her arms stand on end. Marika?

Ylva looked Erik up and down, taking note of his jeans and shoes.

'Are you city folk? Or do you live here too? Are you part of the movement?' she asked.

'We're staying up in the woods in the summer house that belongs to my parents,' said Julia. 'I spent a lot of time here as a child.'

Marika looked older but otherwise much the same, with thick curly hair and eyes that seemed to regard other people with amused curiosity, as if she were speculating about what function they might serve in her life.

They were standing inside the yurt, which was hot and dark. Oriental rugs covered the floor, and there were benches against the walls.

Marika wore a tiny ring in her nose. She had the same freckles she'd had as a child. She gave Julia an enthusiastic hug, with an affected fervour. Julia thought to herself, maybe Marika has become religious. She wondered whether Marika had read her first novel. She tried to recall specific sentences she'd written, but found it impossible.

'You recognise me, don't you?' asked Marika.

'Of course I do,' replied Julia.

They all turned to look at her husband, Chris. He was barefoot, with an open and welcoming expression on his face. When he shook hands with Julia, his handshake was firm, just as it had been a few days earlier.

Marika went to stand next to Chris, leaning against him.

'I can't believe you're here, Julia,' she said. 'When Chris told me he'd invited a couple our age, I wondered if it might be you.'

Julia hadn't thought about Marika in such a long time, and it had never occurred to her that they might run into each other here. As far as Julia knew, Marika's family had stopped spending summers in Mjölkviken sometime in the late nineties.

'Julia and I used to play here as children,' Marika went on. 'She was always so much smarter than me.'

Julia thought Marika was lying in order to flatter her, but the remark had the opposite effect. It sounded condescending.

'And you always had nicer dolls than I did,' said Marika.

Erik gave Marika a hug and seemed cheered by the warm reception.

'It's great to be out here in nature all summer. I'm so tired of the city. Two months here is exactly what I need. I can't understand why we've never come here before,' he said.

'Exactly,' said Marika. 'And now that we've met each other, this could turn out to be really nice.'

For a few seconds no one spoke as they looked around the tent.

'This is amazing,' said Julia, trying to sound sincere.

Marika nodded.

'I saw a tent like this in Scotland and knew at once I had to have one of my own. In certain parts of Finland you can rent yurts, but we wanted to have a permanent one, so Chris built this himself.'

'It's made of nearly all reclaimed materials,' said Chris.

'Where are you from?' asked Erik.

'Scotland,' said Chris.

'So what do you think of Finland?'

'It's wonderful. Reminds me a little of Scotland. A similar mentality. And out here in Mjölkviken … it's so untouched, so peaceful, perfect for the movement.'

Erik asked the same question that had come to Julia.

'What do you mean by the "movement"?'

'I'll explain,' said Chris. 'But first let's sit down and eat.'

It turned out that Marika and Chris were environmental activists. Or rather: they had been. Now they had formed a loose-knit group in Scotland whose purpose – and the whole thing sounded a bit vague to Julia – was to prepare for living in the world after climate change. And they had decided that Mjölkviken was the perfect place from which to welcome the apocalypse.

They learned all of this as they ate dinner down on the beach. Marika had set out large platters of salads on a blanket.

'So what we've discovered lately, over the past five years, is that there is a great pent-up frustration within the environmental movement,' Chris told them with a stern expression as he looked from one guest to another. 'There are thousands of other people out there, first and foremost all the environmental activists, who have reached the same conclusion that I have: that the old type of environmental activism is no longer productive. We'll never be able to change policies by demonstrating outside climate meetings or signing petitions. Fuck that.

It's frustrating and won't lead to anything. That's why we're trying this model instead. And we're not alone. There are other neo-green movements in different parts of the world. We're the Scottish-Nordic version.'

'But what exactly is it you do?' asked Erik.

'You'll see. It's a matter of preparing for disaster before it happens, and it's bound to occur sooner or later. Actually, you might say it has already happened. You can see that clearly in Asia,' said Chris.

Marika glanced at him and he nodded, as if giving her permission to continue where he'd left off.

'It's already too late to do anything politically,' she said. 'It doesn't help if you buy organic tea. That's not going to change anything. So we need to start thinking about how we want our society to be after the disaster. We give seminars, organise workshops, hold meetings, and write and think. But above all, it's a matter of grieving. And realising that the end is already here.'

There were nine people altogether. Marika and Chris, Erik and Julia, Ylva and Roger, the guy with the dreadlocks – his name was Ville – and a young woman named Helena, who was in her twenties and from Greece. She was skinny and dark-haired, wearing a T-shirt with a feminist symbol on the front. She fixed her gaze on Chris as he talked. She spoke fluent English.

Julia tried to remember all their names, but it was difficult. She kept mixing them up but decided that maybe in the long run it didn't matter.

Marika and Chris had a thirteen-year-old son named Leo who attended school in both Finland and Scotland. He didn't say a word as he played solitaire while the grown-ups talked.

When Julia asked Leo whether he liked being in Mjölk-viken, he looked up at her with the same almond-shaped eyes as Marika, but he had clearly inherited some of the unwavering seriousness that characterised his father.

'So where do you actually live?' asked Erik.

'We live in Scotland during the winter months and in Nykarleby in the summer and spring,' said Chris. 'But we're thinking about moving out here.'

'Here?' queried Julia.

'Yes. It would be the perfect place to start a new chapter,' said Chris.

According to Chris, there were thousands of former environmental activists who had joined various so-called 'chapters' all around the world. He talked about Aniara, which was apparently what he'd named his own group, after the epic science fiction poem by the Swedish author Harry Martinson. ('I love Nordic modernism. It's so pure and filled with fresh air,' he said, showing them a well-thumbed copy of the book. 'I always carry it with me.')

'In Martinson's *Aniara*, the earth has been destroyed and a spaceship takes thousands of emigrants to Mars and Venus. But above all, it's a melancholic poem about a lost paradise. It feels like the perfect epic poem for our time,' Chris said.

'So what about the rest of you? Are you also part of the movement?' asked Erik, looking at the others, who had sat in silence as Chris spoke.

Roger was the first to respond. He was now wearing clothes: a pair of corduroy trousers and a big, striped Marimekko shirt that could barely close over his stomach.

'I've been active in Greenpeace for the past twenty years, but then I read Chris's blog and decided to contact him. I was already aware of the movement and similar groups in other places, but I didn't know there were supporters in Finland.'

'I came here with Roger,' said Ylva. 'It's very exciting.'

'How interesting,' said Julia, thinking this really was genuinely interesting because Marika had been such a typical upper-class child. She played piano and seemed to hover above everyone else, yet she'd ended up in this group.

'Is there a specific date?' asked Erik.

'What do you mean?' asked Chris.

'A date when the world will end?'

Marika laughed and glanced at Chris.

'It's not like that at all. It's true that it's too late to turn developments around. We may have as little as ten years before we start seeing huge migrations. Fifteen million people fleeing from Bangladesh alone. North Africa, the Middle East. We're already seeing the beginning of that. But the earth will still exist afterwards. It has survived climate changes before. The question is whether human beings will still exist.'

Now Chris leaned forward.

'Here's the thing: I'm fifty years old, and at that age you inevitably end up a little disillusioned. This is not just about the environment. Over the past few years, politics in the Western world hasn't been exactly encouraging. I'm no longer thinking about joining demonstrations in Paris and hoping for the symbolic power of a protest. Instead, I'm trying to prepare myself for what's coming. Most people are going to be totally unprepared.'

Julia was surprised to hear he was fifty. She would have guessed he was ten years younger. Marika was only a year older than Julia. She was kneeling on the blanket, leaning slightly towards Chris, eating tabbouleh from her plate as Chris talked. The food was good, though not at all what Julia had expected to be eating in Mjölkviken. They had eaten new potatoes and grilled meat all week.

For a few moments no one spoke.

'All of this sounds very exciting,' Erik said at last. 'I mean, it's inspiring, isn't it? I don't understand exactly what you're doing, but it's good you're doing something. I was also thinking of trying to get closer to nature this summer.'

He turned to Julia.

'Right?'

She looked at him without saying a word.

'Yes,' replied Chris. 'Although the point is that we don't think there's anything we can do. We have to accept that there's no hope. Nothing can save us. Or you.'

'Okay, then,' said Erik. 'Let's say that. But at least you make good food, even though you've given up hope for humankind. I really shouldn't eat any more. I was planning on losing some weight and getting into shape this summer.'

Julia looked at him. She thought he was trying to ingratiate himself with Chris, who was so fit. Erik had never mentioned wanting to lose weight.

'Losing weight is the least life-affirming thing anyone can do,' said Ylva, placing her hand on Erik's shoulder.

The evening proceeded with more wine and food. Roger and Ylva suggested that Julia and Erik might want to join them for some skinny-dipping.

'I don't know whether you've ever considered experimenting, but we have a very open relationship,' said Ylva with such a friendly and inviting tone of voice that it sounded as if she were asking them if they'd like dessert.

Julia, who thought the water looked cold, politely declined, and yet she felt a strange sort of envy at Ylva's candid flirtatiousness. Free love seemed to be something that still flourished both in theory and in practice among a number of people of that generation. It was all a little too much for her, and she was glad the children had stayed home.

'I assume that if the world's going to end, it makes no difference who you have sex with,' said Julia. 'Is that true?'

'Sex is never a matter of indifference if you fully enjoy the moment,' said Ylva.

Julia glanced at the boy, Leo, who had been sitting with them the whole time. He remained silent, watching them as if he expected something was about to happen. Roger laughed merrily.

'If desire should arise, we're open to any suggestions.'

Helena, the young Greek woman, still hadn't said much. With studied concentration she had rolled cigarettes, which she then smoked, holding her cigarette between her thumb and index finger, as if sucking on the straw of a milkshake.

'I think it's awesome the way any generational gaps are erased here at Marika and Chris's place,' she said now. 'So what's your thing? What do you believe?'

'Our thing?' asked Julia.

'You haven't really said. Do you belong to those who still think that traditional parliamentary democracy will somehow magically make the polar ice caps stop melting?'

'I haven't actually thought about that. But I assume there's no harm in voting green,' said Julia. 'It has to be better than nothing, right?'

Helena laughed.

'Ah. So you're one of those. A little recycling and we've solved all the problems. Just read a few articles and share them on Facebook. People in Iraq, who are already being persecuted by ISIS, die from heat waves while you think it's lovely that the summer here in Finland is a little warmer. You're in for a big surprise,' she said, speaking English with an American accent.

Julia looked at her and suddenly felt sad. She thought this sort of guilt-tripping reminded her of what she'd experienced in other situations, other relationships. Placing blame on someone else was a means of strengthening your own convictions.

'But if you say there's no longer anything to be done, why

can't you just go on living like before? What does it matter if you're unaware?'

'I choose instead to take the red pill. I want to see how deep the rabbit hole is,' said Helena.

'Sorry?' said Julia.

'*The Matrix*. Right?' said Erik.

Helena nodded, looking pleased. Julia gave Erik a puzzled look.

'Keanu Reeves has to choose between the red and the blue pill. If he takes the blue pill, he'll wake up in his own bed the next day and everything will be the way it was before. If he takes the red pill, he'll get to see the truth. We saw the film at the cinema before the kids were born.'

Helena laughed and went back to sucking on her cigarette.

Eventually the men went off to heat up the sauna. Julia stayed sitting on the blanket with Marika while the others dispersed. It had been more than twenty years since they'd last seen each other, but Julia noticed that her friend could still provoke the same feelings in her – the sense that Marika had an emotional advantage over her. She had grown more beautiful over the years, but mostly she seemed just the same.

'Where did you and Chris meet?' asked Julia. She poured herself another glass of wine. Marika pulled her hair back from her face.

'We met at a seminar on de-civilisation in Oslo.'

'De-what?'

'Not sure what it's called in Swedish, but in English it's "de-civilisation", a rather loosely used term. But that's not the point. I was there because I was curious. I'd taken a few months off from work to recharge my batteries, so to speak, and that's when I met Chris. It was an intellectual attraction. Maybe you know what I mean? As if we'd met before.'

Julia nodded and sipped her wine. 'What kind of work do you do?' she asked.

'I'm actually a botanist. I've worked in the profession off and on over the years. But right now I'm involved in the movement.'

'I assume botanists will also be needed when the climate goes to hell,' said Julia, laughing.

'Well, that depends how bad it gets. What do you do, by the way?'

'I write. Or try to write. I'm working on a novel.'

'So you're an author? How did you happen to decide to do that?'

Julia thought that maybe she was a writer because of people like Marika, people who had affected her during childhood, who had left traces behind, experiences that Julia wanted to return to, in the same way as she had returned to Mjölkviken in her first book.

'Well … I have a job at the university too, teaching a few courses. And I've already written one novel.'

'Oh, I should read it. I don't read much, but Chris has a blog. I think blogs are great because they're interactive. You get in touch with other people and you can exchange ideas. You can't do that with a traditional book,' said Marika.

'My first novel was nominated for the Runeberg literary prize.'

'Wow,' said Marika, nodding pensively. 'Is there an English translation? These days I prefer reading English.'

'Yes, actually, there is,' said Julia.

'I'll have to check that out sometime. I have a Kindle. Maybe I can download it this summer.'

Julia regretted saying anything about her book. She didn't want Marika to read it, even though it was fiction, even though it was about something that happened so many years ago. It made her feel so naked, so absurd.

'What kind of work does your husband do?' asked Marika.

'Erik? Oh, he's in IT. For a long time he had his own firm, but then he was hired by a big company in Helsinki.'

Julia noticed that she was bragging. There was something about Marika that brought out that side of her. She didn't want to say that Erik was the IT manager of a department store. In Marika's world, that would undoubtedly sound far from sexy. Her husband Chris had talked about 'zero growth' and such things all evening. These were people who were privileged enough to condemn consumption. Yet she had never imagined that Marika would become an activist or anything like that. Instead, she'd always thought – when they were kids – that Marika would follow in her parents' footsteps and become a doctor or go into some other highly bourgeois profession.

'So what are your parents doing these days?' asked Julia.

'Pappa lives in Åbo. He's remarried. Mamma died from uterine cancer five years ago. I don't see Pappa very often. You know, over the past few years I've had occasion to think about my childhood. Chris says it was a destructive childhood, that my parents were emotionally immature. Now that Pappa has met another woman, I no longer feel like he's my responsibility. I notice that I'm happier when we're not in contact,' she said.

Julia found this surprising. She had always envied Marika, who seemed to have a symbiotic relationship with her parents. They were the perfect little family, beautiful and gentle, and their home always smelled so good.

'I bet the sauna is heated up by now,' said Marika. 'It'll be almost like when we were kids.'

Marika lay down on the top bench in the sauna. She stretched out full length, resting her head on a towel.

'What do you think about Chris?'

They had undressed in the small room where the towels

hung on hooks, and Julia had caught a glimpse of Marika's body. She was slender and athletic.

'What do you mean?' asked Julia.

'I don't know. I was just wondering what sort of impression he makes.'

'He seems nice.'

'Really? He's terribly ambitious. He always does everything a hundred per cent. He's totally focused. I'm so glad we met. He's a man I can truly admire,' she said.

Julia thought this might be the way women were expected to talk in a sauna about their husbands.

'How did you meet Erik?' asked Marika.

'We've known each other for a thousand years,' said Julia. It usually sounded funny when she said that, but for some reason it didn't this time. 'He's a fantastic father,' she added.

'I never thought I'd end up with such an alpha male as Chris,' said Marika. 'In fact, I lived with a woman for almost three years while I was studying at the university. I threw my whole self into that identity. I really thought I was a lesbian. When I met Chris it was like I'd found something I'd always been looking for. Almost as if someone finally took my hand and led me straight into the woods, if you get what I mean.'

Julia found the analogy odd. It made it sound as if Marika was still lost. Maybe that's how people expressed themselves in blogs.

'Is there any sort of feminist perspective in the whole thing?' asked Julia.

'What do you mean?'

'I mean, if you're thinking we're going to return to a pre-industrial society, there's a risk that it'll be a step back for equality. Are you picturing that women will do the cooking while the men go out and hunt?'

'I've never thought about it that way,' said Marika. 'But I think people can be equal even if you're not anthropocentric. I think that's how Chris looks at it too. He's given a lot of thought to how society could be better organised.'

'I'm sure he has,' said Julia, hearing at once the sarcasm in her voice.

But Marika didn't seem to react.

'So what are you writing now?' she asked.

'Oh, it's nothing … or rather, it's a historical novel that takes place in Jakobstad.'

And the second she said that, she had an idea. In her mind she pictured her characters – as she sometimes did in the most unexpected situations – and she knew exactly what she was going to write the next day. She knew how it related to the way she felt about Marika, an insight into the way small towns were marked by class hierarchies. For her, this book project was important; it was anchored in her family history, in her own background, in what had gone on before her parents' generation. But it was difficult, considerably more difficult than she had imagined, to write about a historical era that she'd seen only in photographs. What did she know about how her maternal grandmother regarded her job, or life in general?

'It sounds exciting. And challenging,' said Marika.

'It is. I don't know what I'm thinking until I actually write down the words. But maybe I've always been like that. I need to write down a thought before I know what I think.'

'Chris says that one problem with human civilisation is that we've learned to break down things rationally and put everything into complicated systems, when we should be listening much more to our inner instincts. People in a hunter-gatherer society were in many ways happier than we are,' said Marika.

Julia wondered if that could be true. But she didn't say anything, merely looking at the sauna heating unit and the steam rising from the stones after she tossed water onto them. She could feel the steam burning her back.

'Shall we go down to the beach?' asked Marika.

2

ALICE SAT ACROSS FROM Anton drinking beer. She had opened one of their father's beer cans after their parents left and filled a couple of coffee cups, which she'd taken from the kitchen cupboard.

The pale yellow beer foamed in the cups. Anton had taken a small sip, but it was bitter and lukewarm and impossible to drink. Instead, he was eating crisps that they'd bought at the supermarket earlier in the day.

'What shall we do?' he asked. He hoped Alice was in a good mood. He knew that he didn't deserve any attention from her because he teased her so often. He would pinch and hit her, but somehow she always seemed to forgive him.

He could often tell in advance when he was about to lose control. It actually made him feel good, so that's why he usually let it happen. There was a sense of liberation and joy at finding out what might occur when he allowed his rage to bubble to the surface and set off a chain of events. Yet afterwards he always felt ashamed, and sometimes he wondered whether there was something wrong with him because he couldn't control his moods. He didn't know of anyone else in his class who behaved the way he did.

Right now he didn't want Alice to get angry, so he kept quiet and fixed his eyes on her. She was drinking steadily, focusing all her attention on the beer without answering his question.

'Do you want to play cards?' he asked cautiously.

She looked at him. Her black fringe hung in her face, making her eyes look like stones in a well.

'Could we go back to the woods?' she asked.

'Okay,' he said. 'Do you want the rest of my beer?'

She took his cup and drank almost all of it.

'Come on,' she said and then stood up.

They walked down to the glade where they'd found the tadpoles. Anton had brought along the bag of crisps, which he ate as he walked beside Alice. When they reached the pool of water, she leaned down and scooped away the leaves.

'I'll give you ten euros if you swallow a tadpole,' she said.

'Not in a million years,' said Anton.

He set the bag of crisps on the ground. It was hot out here in the glade. The slender trunks of the pines seemed redder than before. The rocky ground felt smooth underfoot, though it was wet in the small crevices. When he stuck his hand into bigger grooves, he noticed that the water was lukewarm because it had been sitting in the sun all day.

Anton pushed some leaves aside with his hand and saw a tadpole swiftly swim for a cleft in the rock wall, but it got stuck, its little tail flailing. It was a dark-brown-green colour, almost black. Anton reached down and scooped it up.

'Look at this!'

'Great!' said Alice. 'Are you sure you don't want to eat one of them?'

'Yuck,' said Anton, imagining how slimy it would feel in his mouth.

They caught five tadpoles in half an hour and took several pictures with Alice's mobile phone as the tiny creatures lay wriggling on the ground.

When they finished taking pictures, they heard laughter

echoing from the shore.

'Want to go and spy on them?' asked Alice.

Anton nodded because he felt such a longing to see his mother.

The sounds from the party swept through the woods like gentle notes above the rushing of the sea.

'Okay,' said Alice. 'Let's go.'

The alcohol had pleasantly erased all contours in the world, so it took a while before Alice noticed the dead moose.

The head was sticking out between two tree trunks, leaning slightly to one side. The eye sockets were empty and black, as if the eyes had sunk back inside the skull. Alice could see bits of the skeleton exposed in the forehead and close to the muzzle.

Anton stopped next to her and took her hand.

'Wait here,' she said.

She moved closer. The rest of the enormous body was slumped behind the tree, hollowed out and red.

'It must have got its head stuck between the trees,' she said. 'And then it died.'

'It stinks,' said Anton.

Only now did Alice notice the smell coming from the animal's body, an intense, sweet smell. The remaining patches of dark pelt looked dry and shiny. On parts of the body the fur had been eaten away. The front part of the moose looked as if it were wedged tight, as if it had jumped up in the tree and got caught.

Alice pushed back a wave of nausea. Yet there was something fascinating, almost majestic, about this animal, the fact that it was so hideous and so raw.

'Are you scared?' she asked Anton.

He shook his head.

Alice could hear her own breathing as she got out her mobile and snapped a picture. On Instagram she chose the filter Lark and wrote: '#corpse #scary #woods #moose #shithappens'.

Anton's heart beat faster as they walked the last part of the way. He wasn't scared, that was the wrong word, but he was eager to talk about what they'd just seen.

They followed the sound of the sea down to the road. They walked past the car park, which looked abandoned. It was covered with pine needles and piles of leaves. The asphalt had cracked in places, and weeds had sprouted up.

When they reached the neighbours' property, they found all the grown-ups sitting on a blanket. They were talking loudly and laughing. Several grown-ups were unfamiliar, and Anton immediately regretted coming here. He wasn't keen on interrupting their festivities.

His mother looked like a different person as she talked to the others. She looked so alert, and now he'd be forced to yank her away from the situation, almost like waking someone who's been asleep.

Alice made the first move.

'Pappa, we found something in the woods,' she said.

Their parents now caught sight of them. At first they looked surprised, then their father smiled, a gentle and easy smile, as if suddenly remembering who they were.

'We found a moose!' said Anton, going over to his mother and sitting down next to her.

All the others stopped talking, and Anton wished he hadn't said anything. Now they expected him to say more.

There was a boy with the group. He was sitting on one corner of the blanket, giving Anton an enquiring look. He seemed to be about the same age as Alice. Suddenly Anton felt ridiculous about his eager announcement.

'A moose? Did it run away?' asked Julia.

'No, it's hanging in a tree. It's dead,' said Alice.

'Ugh. Where was it?' asked one of the women.

'In the woods, not far from our house. It looks like it's been there a long time. It smells,' said Alice, glancing at the boy sitting on the blanket.

'Should we go and have a look?' asked their father.

'I'm sure it will still be there tomorrow. If it's dead, there's not much we can do, anyway,' said Julia.

Anton looked at her, surprised to hear how unaffected she seemed. As if she'd rather stay here with all these strangers.

'I'll go with you tomorrow. Then we'll see what we can do,' said one of the men in English. Anton recognised him. He was the man who had turned up at the tennis court a few days ago.

Alice was now staring at the boy with interest. When he glanced at her, she lowered her eyes. He had blond hair and was wearing a blue T-shirt and a pair of Converse trainers, just like Alice. He looks a little stuck-up, thought Anton, as if he's the sort of person who might say something mean in the school-yard. Anton was used to hearing those kinds of remarks. Once he'd been wearing a T-shirt with a Disney image on the front, and he heard an older boy say it was a girl's T-shirt. When he got home, Anton took off the shirt, crumpled it into a ball, and hid it at the back of the wardrobe. One day his mother found the shirt, washed it, and then put it back with the rest of his clothes. So he threw the shirt into the big rubbish bin in the yard.

'Maybe you kids could find something to do together,' suggested his mother now.

That was exactly what Anton had feared. That he and Alice would be forced to hang out with this boy they didn't know.

Alice glanced down at her phone.

'This is Alice,' their mother was saying. 'Go and shake hands with Leo,' she told Alice.

Alice stuck her phone in her pocket and went over where the boy was sitting.

'Hi,' he said.

'Say your name when you greet people,' said the English-speaking man, whom Anton assumed must be the boy's father.

'Leo,' said the boy, and they shook hands.

They got some ice cream, and Anton ate it sitting next to his mother on the blanket.

'When are we going home?' he asked her. The moose in the woods made him uneasy and he was cold. He knew Alice would tell the new boy that they should go back to have a look at the dead moose. He didn't want to do that.

'We've only been here a little while. I think we'll be taking another sauna later. Maybe you kids would like to go swimming afterwards?' said his mother.

'But the water is so cold,' Anton replied.

'Not after the sauna,' said his father.

'I think it's too cold,' said Anton. He looked at the grown-ups seated around him and thought how peculiar they were. Much more peculiar than the people his parents usually spent time with.

After finishing their ice cream, Alice asked Leo – just as Anton had predicted – whether he wanted to go to the woods with them to see the moose. Anton hesitated. He didn't want to stay here with these peculiar grown-ups, but he didn't want to see the moose again. He didn't want to smell its rotting body and imagine all the maggots crawling around inside. He didn't want to revisit that place without his parents.

But when Alice and Leo headed off, Erik told Anton to go with them.

'Just think what a luxury it is for you kids to run around freely out here with no one hovering over you. Isn't that exciting? To be out here in nature? Run along and play, Anton. And you can stay up as late as you like tonight. I promise. There are no rules here,' he said.

Erik looked around. He seemed pleased with what he'd said, as if he'd been speaking just as much to the others as to his son.

'Well, maybe not as late as you want. And you need to be careful about going into the water. I don't want you venturing out onto any dangerous rocks,' said Julia.

'Okay. No dangerous rocks. And don't go so far away that you can't hear us if we call. I don't think we'll be staying real late,' said Erik.

This time Anton was the first to see the moose. It didn't seem as scary as when they'd discovered it.

'Check this out,' he said, speaking suddenly with a slight accent, as if subconsciously trying to mimic Leo's way of talking. He wondered whether Alice noticed.

'Fuck,' said Leo, going over to the animal. It looked different now that Anton was seeing it for the second time. It was even more disgusting than he remembered, now that he inspected it more closely. There was also something unsettling about this place: the quiet and stillness of the woods surrounding them, the fact that all these animals lived here, yet they never saw any of them.

Leo poked at the body.

'Do you think I could have the head, once they pull it loose? It would be cool to take it home. Once, in Scotland, I saw somebody hang a dead cat from the ceiling, like a lamp.'

'I can ask Pappa to save it for you,' said Alice.

'But why is it hanging there like that?' asked Leo. 'The body has to be at least a metre off the ground. Do you think someone lifted it up there?'

Anton suddenly had a bad feeling. He pictured somebody

first killing the moose and then hanging it up in the tree.

'Maybe it jumped up to catch something and got caught,' suggested Alice.

For thirty seconds none of them spoke. Anton was thinking of asking the others what they wanted to do – maybe they could play cards? – but he didn't dare.

'Do you want a beer?' Alice said at last.

'A beer?' Leo repeated.

'Pappa has lots of cases of beer. We can go up to the house and share one. Or you can have a whole can for yourself, if you want.'

'Sure, that sounds good.'

Anton broke off a long tree branch and walked down to the tarn. He stuck the branch in the water to see how deep it was. Alice and Leo had each fetched a beer and were sitting in the yard. The branch turned out to be too short. It didn't touch the bottom even when Anton leaned so far forward that he almost fell off the rock he was standing on.

When he got tired of trying, he walked back up to the house. Leo and Alice had started piling up branches near the open fire pit.

'We're thinking of lighting a fire. Want to help?' said Alice.

Anton went with them to look for branches and kindling. They soon had a big pile. The woods behind the house were overgrown and filled with dead evergreens with branches that were easy to break off. Leo lit the fire. Then he and Alice sat down with their beers and stared at the flames while Anton sat across from them. The fire crackled and smelled of charred wood.

'I love being here,' Alice said suddenly. 'Right this minute, at least. It's great. And I love this beer.'

'How long are you staying? All summer?' asked Leo. It made

Anton feel as if somehow he already knew Leo, as if they'd always spent their summers here together.

'Until school starts,' she said.

'My parents think I should quit school so they can home-school me here. Actually, they'd like me to attend a Steiner school, but there aren't any around here.'

A few of Anton's former pre-school classmates went to a Steiner school. He'd heard that there were no textbooks, except for ones the students made themselves. They played the kantele in music class, and they made artwork from things they found in the woods.

'I want another one. How about you?' asked Leo, looking at his beer can.

The shadows cast by the fire made his face seem in constant motion, even though his eyes weren't moving at all. His eyes made Anton think of a fox or a cat.

'I don't think you should take any more of Pappa's beer,' said Anton. 'He'll notice.'

'Oh, Anton, don't be a baby,' said Alice.

'Do you think he keeps track of how many cans he has?' asked Leo.

'Well, if half the cans in the case are gone ...' said Anton.

Alice rolled her eyes. She seemed different now, not as quiet and withdrawn as she normally was around other people. Not shy or timid. She tucked her hair behind her ear, exposing her neck, so that Leo would notice. They were both staring into the fire as if wondering what their next move would be. The mood made Anton nervous. He wished Leo wasn't their neighbour, because now the balance had been upset.

'Do you have a lot of friends back in Helsinki?' Leo asked Alice.

Anton could have answered that question. He could have said that Alice didn't have a boyfriend, that she'd never been interested in having one, that she mostly stayed in her room and checked her phone and listened to boring music. But Leo would probably find out all that for himself.

'Why don't you go see if there's any booze in the house?' Leo said to Anton. 'Whisky or gin or anything like that.'

'Please?' said Alice. She looked at her brother and motioned towards the house. Anton was more than happy to leave. The fire was burning his face, and he was tired of Alice and Leo and the way they spoke to each other.

But there wasn't much to do back at the house, so he started thinking of his mother again. He glanced at the clock and saw it was only nine thirty. They might be staying late over at the neighbours' place, maybe until midnight. He wasn't proud of the way he was feeling. He had a lump in his throat, and he tried to swallow to make it go away, but that didn't help. He stood in the kitchen for several seconds, trying to make the lump disappear. He was almost panic-stricken. He couldn't open his mouth, but finally he inhaled through his nose and then went over to the worktop to fetch a glass of water. He quickly drank the whole glass.

He opened the cupboard where his parents kept the bottles of booze. There were only two. One held a clear liquid. The other held something yellow, and it said BACARDI GOLD on the label. He picked up that bottle and filled two glasses. The alcohol had a beautiful amber colour, and he leaned close to take a sniff. It smelled awful, but he decided to have a sip, trying not to think about how much he swallowed. It burned his throat, so intense and powerful, and he felt the heat run down to his stomach. He couldn't help coughing, and his eyes filled with tears. Anton thought it was crazy that the grown-ups would drink this stuff voluntarily, but maybe it was like his father said: that there were certain things only grown-ups understood.

Leo's face brightened when he saw Anton coming across the yard carrying a glass in each hand.

'Christ, you really poured a lot in each glass,' he said. 'We're going to be totally gone. My father drinks this much, but he's used to it.'

'Does your father drink a lot?' asked Alice.

'He drinks, he smokes grass. He says there's nothing he hasn't tried in his life, except for heroin. Mamma says it was a shock for him to have a kid. Then he had to become an adult with responsibilities. He had to calm down.'

'Our parents got drunk once,' said Alice.

'When?' asked Anton with interest.

'Once when you were younger. It was the first of May, at a party with the neighbours. Pappa started singing and shouting. So they must have been drunk.'

Anton thought about this. He'd never seen his parents behave differently. Sometimes they smelled of wine, but that was all. It sounded so strange to hear Leo talking about his father like that. It opened a chasm that Anton didn't really want to see. Leo didn't seem to think there was anything strange about it.

'Geez, this is strong,' said Alice.

'I think it's great!' said Leo.

Anton sat on the other side of the fire, staring at them. After a while a strange silence came over them. Alice slowly leaned towards Leo until she fell against him.

'Sorry!' she said. 'I think I'm a little drunk.'

She stood up and started flapping her arms.

'Ohhh … I'm drunk! Drunk, drunk, drunk!'

Leo looked at her and laughed.

'Want to go swimming?' she asked cheerfully.

3

THE WATER WAS COLD, but Alice didn't care, because so much was going on inside her body. She moved slowly, languidly, like in a film, as if surrounded by some sort of membrane that protected her from everything. She'd changed into her swimsuit in the sauna guestroom, wrapping a big towel around her. She waded into the water until it reached to her stomach, then she paused, waiting for the right moment to simply let go and allow herself to float. It suddenly felt so enticing compared with a week ago. She thought now that she loved being in Mjölkviken.

Leo was behind her. He was sweet, but that wasn't the main thing. Maybe, instead, it was the way he looked at her. No one had ever looked at her like that before, or talked to her that way. To avoid his eyes, she stared straight ahead at the horizon. His gaze was too intense, too interested, as if he lacked the normal distance that most people maintained with one another. They'd known each other only a few hours, yet he talked as if he'd always known her. What was that about?

Suddenly she thought of the gold ring she'd found on the first day. She decided to show it to Leo when they went back.

He'd said they should stay up to watch the sunset, and he knew of a special place out on the rocks. He hadn't asked her if she wanted to do this; he seemed to assume she would say yes.

'It's ice cold,' he said now, but she didn't turn around. She heard him speaking behind her, his voice like fine sandpaper.

She threw herself into the water, wanting to show him that she too could take the initiative and act spontaneously. It was so easy, so simple, and the water was so clear. She ducked her head under and swam a few strokes, opening her eyes to peer down at the soft, sandy bottom, which was a bit blurry, even though she could almost touch it.

Leo was now swimming alongside her.

'Is your hair really black?' he asked.

All of a sudden she was aware of her appearance, her small breasts, her flabby arms. She touched her hair plastered against her face like a wet rag.

'I dyed it,' she said.

He nodded.

She wondered what he was thinking.

She was convinced that then and there he'd decided she was too childish and immature. Maybe he knew girls who had already done it.

'Do you think it's possible to drown yourself?'

Now they were both standing up. The water reached to his waist.

'Maybe. If you threw yourself into a river. There was some author who did that,' she said.

'A girl in my class lay down on the railway tracks last spring. She wanted to kill herself, but her mother came and dragged her away. She did it again, a week later, and that time she died.'

Alice wondered if he was telling the truth. Maybe he was the sort of person who made up things like that. But when she glanced at him, his eyes looked sorrowful and his gaze was fixed on a faraway spot on the horizon.

'Why did she do it?'

'My mother says it was a cry for help. Meaning that she didn't really want to kill herself. She wanted somebody to notice that she was having a bad time. She was always like that, saying that she wanted to kill herself. But I never thought she'd actually do it.'

'Did you know her?'

'Not really. I was going out with her friend. We're not together any more.'

Alice had never had a boyfriend, and she didn't think she ever would. But maybe it was easier for him, since he'd already had a girlfriend. She felt a great longing in her gut. She touched his ear, wiping away a drop of water.

'Was it fun?'

'What?'

'Being together?'

'It was okay,' he said, shrugging.

They didn't feel like swimming any more. They sat on the beach and stared at the horizon, wrapped in the towels they'd brought. Anton stood a short distance away, skimming stones. He hadn't gone swimming, merely watched them from the shore as he restlessly roamed over the rocks, like a dog who worries his master might drown.

'Alice, can we go back to the house now?' he asked.

'Soon,' said Alice.

'Do you have a sauna?' asked Leo.

'Sure, but it takes a long time to heat up,' she said.

'Oh,' said Leo, and for some reason Alice felt disappointed. Maybe he didn't mean for them to take a sauna together, but it was possible that's what he was thinking. She wondered why she didn't feel embarrassed at the thought. Under normal circumstances she would have been terrified to take a sauna with a boy other than Anton.

She was still dizzy from all the alcohol. It was a warm feeling, in every way a much better feeling than she'd expected. She thought to herself: I could get used to this. Such joy, such a sense that all my problems have disappeared, a giddiness in my stomach and head, and feeling like I'm really here, in the present moment.

They heard giggling and a muted splashing from the opposite shore. Two grown-ups had jumped into the water.

'Is that your mother?' asked Alice.

'Where?' said Leo.

'Both of our mothers. They're in the water, swimming.'

Alice assumed they'd been in the sauna and afterwards had gone straight down to the water. Her mother's dark hair floated on the surface as she swam. She was totally focused on her strokes. She did everything like that, with great purpose and concentration, always looking so pretty. She swam like someone who did so often.

The other woman swam behind her. Then both of them paused and floated for a moment, looking at each other. Alice turned away. It seemed too private. Why were grown-ups always like that? Why did they look like strangers when seen from a distance, losing all sense of dignity? Leo's mother raised her hand and quickly placed it on top of Julia's head. Maybe she's swatting away a mosquito, thought Alice. But her mother did the same thing, just for a second, and then both women dived back into the water and swam for shore. They got out and picked up their towels.

Leo got up and dried himself off, as if the whole scene bored him. He looked at the sky and came over to Alice. Strange how tanned he was, even though the summer hadn't been very good so far. His body was thin, his arms sinewy. Alice pictured him running through the woods, climbing trees, playing football, as if he were a wilder and freer child than any she'd ever met in Helsinki. And maybe he was, maybe that's why he talked in such a natural and unafraid way.

He didn't seem to need any time to gather his thoughts before speaking. He would merely look at her with those eyes that were as clear as the water they'd been swimming in. Greenish-blue eyes.

'Alice, have you ever played Pidro?'

'No … What's that?'

'A card game that a lot of people play here in Ostrobothnia. I think it originated in Argentina. I can teach you. Shall we go back to the house?'

'Okay,' she said, thinking that she loved him. Was that even possible after only a few hours?

4

SOMETIME DURING THE EVENING Erik decided to
let it all go. To stop worrying about his job, to stop thinking that
he needed to come up with something interesting to contribute
to Chris's discussions about the climate, to drop the idea that
everything would work out. He took off his sport coat and
socks and lay down on the blanket where they'd eaten dinner.
The idealism of these people reminded him of how things used
to be, how he used to be, when he'd had a vision of his own,
maybe not the same one these people had, and yet he'd believed
in something. Once upon a time he'd been twenty-two years
old and he believed that his future would be about creating a
successful mobile phone game for the world market. But that's
not how things had turned out.

It was uncertain whether Erik would be able to find a new
job in the next six months. All week long, he'd sat on the rocks
outside the summer house, checking online for job announcements, but nothing seemed interesting or promising. IT-support
for a secondary school in Lovisa? Child-care in Esbo? Manager
of digital media for a newspaper? He was either over- or under-
qualified for all the jobs.

The others had been taking turns in the sauna. Now he lay
here feeling the sand between his toes as he listened to them
talking about climate change.

Erik realised how little he really knew about the topic. Alice sometimes made the rest of the family feel guilty because they didn't sort the rubbish carefully enough. Yet personally he'd never really given much thought to the environment.

Erik liked to think of himself as a progressive optimist, but lately it felt like everyone around him had become pessimists. The climate crisis, the financial crisis, the refugee crisis, the euro crisis, the newspaper crisis, the crisis in Ukraine, in the EU, the crisis within the Social Democratic party ... There was no area of society that wasn't in crisis. And in Finland people were especially good at crises, as if they didn't feel truly comfortable unless everything was going to hell.

'There's no chance we'll be able to meet the two-degree goal, and even if we managed to achieve a globally binding agreement, the reality is that we're talking about up to six degrees. And then it's sayonara to all of us,' said Helena. She was looking very intent and serious, yet she seemed to be speaking directly to Chris, as if trying to impress him with her rhetoric.

They'd had more dessert. Biscuits with a special kind of tea, which Chris said was supposed to be mind-expanding, and everyone except Julia had said yes. Erik thought the tea tasted bitter, but nevertheless he'd finished off a whole cup.

Ylva and Roger had gone into the house, apparently to have sex (great for the digestion!), but they'd promised to come back later. Marika and Julia were down at the beach, swimming.

'James Hansen recently wrote that global warming will already start accelerating exponentially at 1.5 degrees, which means that it won't matter whether we manage to keep to two degrees,' Helena went on. Everyone agreed, though a bit distractedly, as if the subject had been discussed many times before. Chris sat on the blanket with a stoic expression, like a prophet taking a momentary break from issuing predictions.

Erik thought about how different these people were from his colleagues at the department store. When Erik was studying at the University of Technology, he'd known idealists. The whole atmosphere had been idealistic during those first years. His former colleague Martin had been a communist-oriented computer programmer who talked about Marx at the same time as he planned to earn his first million before he turned twenty-five. Now Martin was one of Finland's wealthiest individuals under forty, and he possessed some of the same charisma as Chris. Martin's success irritated Erik, mostly because he could have been in the same situation if only he hadn't given up the uncertain path of a start-up entrepreneur. But that was part of the agreement he'd made with Julia when the kids were young: he would get a regular job with a monthly salary, and she would be allowed to write. He'd been reminded of Martin only last week when a reporter from an evening newspaper had phoned to ask him about Martin's wild youth. Erik had done his best not to sound bitter or jealous of his former colleague.

Now Helena was talking about climate scientists that he'd never heard of, about how the water from the polar ice could create totally unforeseen chain reactions, and about grasshoppers as a source of protein.

Erik looked up from where he was lying on the blanket and thought that in spite of everything, it all seemed so far away right now, here on the shore of this beautiful, quiet bay. The air was cool and clear. He gazed at the horizon and tried to imagine what it would be like if the water rose several metres.

He sat up and tucked his feet under him.

'So what do you think we should do?' he asked.

The others turned to him, as if Erik's question was both unexpected and confrontational.

'What do you mean by "do"?' asked Helena. 'That's an awfully broad question.'

Chris hadn't said anything for a while, merely nodding during the conversation, looking amused. But now he decided to speak.

'There's nothing to do. We're a tiny vessel floating in space and no one can hear us scream,' he said.

Erik thought that sounded very cryptic.

Helena nodded agreement.

'New York, Los Angeles, Barcelona, all the coastal areas will be hit first. Not to mention the small islands that are already threatening to disappear. The Maldives, Tuvalu,' said Chris, ticking them off one by one.

Ville sat nearby, smoking and staring at the small fire they had lit. He looked amused, as if he was actually looking forward to the disaster.

'But what about in the meantime?' Erik went on. 'I mean, shouldn't we try to do something to prevent it? Even if the earth ends in a hundred years, daily life is continuing right now, with everything that involves. I can't go to the bank and say that I want to stop making payments because Helsinki will soon be underwater ... I mean ...'

He lost the thread of his argument. It was as if his tongue had got tangled up in the words.

Chris gave him an amused look. 'In fact,' he said, 'there are insurance companies that are making money on doing climate analyses. Lots of people are already getting rich off the whole thing. You have no idea.'

Helena leaned towards Chris and stroked his chest.

Erik must have nodded off because when he looked up again he saw Julia and Marika coming up from the beach. They each had a towel wrapped around them, and water was dripping from their bodies. Marika looked very fit, but not in a deliberate sort of way. It seemed to be her natural body type, as if she enjoyed exercising and maybe even showing off her figure. She took off the towel and stood naked in front of the others as she dried her face.

'I think I'll go back in the sauna,' she said. 'Anybody want to join me?'

'I'll come and get warmed up for a while,' said Julia, and they both headed off.

Chris got out a bottle of Scotch and filled several worn glasses he'd brought from the kitchen. Erik took a sip and felt the heat spread down his throat and into his stomach. He thought about the children and wondered where they were right now. Presumably they'd gone back to the summer house or were somewhere out on the rocks. It's good for them to run free, he thought, feeling almost jealous. Oh, to be a child again without any worries.

'It's time for us to get ready for the big bonfire,' said Chris. 'Helena, Ville, could you gather up the rubbish, so we can burn it in the fire?'

Helena and Ville got up and began walking around the yard, collecting anything that could be burned. Erik stayed sitting on the blanket with Chris. He drank slowly from his glass.

'So tell me how you got involved in the environmental movement,' said Erik.

Chris leaned back with a small smile, as if that was a question he'd been asked many times before, and he enjoyed answering it.

Erik stared at the glow from the fire, which looked as if it were lighting up the whole beach. He seemed to see a microcosm, a small solar system within the fire itself.

Chris rubbed his hands and used a stick to poke at the fire, making it crackle. An explosion of colours appeared before Erik's eyes.

Chris said, 'I suppose it started when I was a boy. My father loved going hiking, and I was an only child, so it was easy for him to take me along. We hiked a lot in the Scottish highlands, sometimes spending weeks in the summertime on lengthy expeditions. It was a very special sort of upbringing, because my father didn't talk much. So we'd be hiking on some mountain, and neither of us would say a word for several hours. After a while, you develop a different perspective, you become more aware of what is happening around you. How the wind is blowing, all the scents, the birds singing. At least that's how it was for me. I began to understand that nature is totally independent, it doesn't rely on human beings, it's indifferent to us. Later, when I got older, I started travelling to different places in the world, which merely reinforced this feeling I had. I think a lot of climate activists don't have a particularly close relationship to nature. For them, it's more about human beings.'

Erik nodded. He thought he could suddenly picture what Chris meant. He could feel the wind blowing, he heard how it actually sounded in his ears, like a voice, as if it were whispering to him.

'So you're saying that it's selfish to try and save the planet, which is a human way of thinking?' he said, feeling as if he'd suddenly had an epiphany.

Chris smiled.

'Absolutely true. A lot of activists think that we'll be able to live well in the future if only we put our efforts into wind energy and low-energy lights and do some recycling. But it's already too late for all that. Folks in the environmental movement don't want to hear that, because it's viewed as counterproductive, as if we're taking away their last hope. Some people among them have even started talking about nuclear energy and solutions that might appeal to the right-wing. For me, it's not a question of right-wing or left-wing. My sense of the world has more to do with the magic of nature, if that doesn't sound too pretentious. It's about holding on to a small part of that magic. Nature will continue to exist, even without us. Maybe it would be just as well if human beings were obliterated,' he said.

Erik listened in silence. He thought he might actually be able to understand how enticing that was. To renounce civilisation. But it seemed so short-sighted. If that's what you decided today, you still had a life to live tomorrow. And for that you needed to get money from somewhere.

Yet he felt that his personal reservations were starting to be dispelled. Chris's voice sounded more and more convincing.

Helena and Ville came back to the blanket and sat down.

'I think we're ready now,' said Helena.

Chris leaned forward, raised his glass of whisky, and looked at it without responding.

He glanced at Erik and took his hand.

'Erik, I'm not saying we shouldn't give a damn about anything. At the same time, we shouldn't pretend that we're not in despair. We're all in despair,' he said, without releasing his grip.

Erik wanted to look away, but he couldn't. There was something about Chris's expression that mesmerised him.

Finally Chris let go of Erik's hand and continued: 'What I've been feeling lately is a great sense of sorrow. I'm grieving. I'm tired. And that's what our movement is really about – accepting the grief instead of talking about hope all the time. Hope is a completely meaningless concept.'

'Exactly,' said Helena.

Erik thought about this. Suddenly his job at the department store seemed so petty. What did quarterly reports and business expansion matter when an entire cosmos could be found in the flames of a fire? He felt an urge to phone Jouni and tell him that he didn't care about being given the sack because he wanted to get out of the rat race.

'It's also about injustices,' said Helena. 'The fact that the countries which produce the biggest percentage of emissions don't take responsibility. It's the poorest countries that suffer the most, and yet they didn't cause the problem. That's a discussion we also need to have.'

Chris didn't seem to agree.

'A discussion about global politics doesn't belong here.

What I'm trying to say is that I'm not interested in politics. Some people take the view that it's bourgeois to talk about the intrinsic value of nature. That it's something the middle-class can afford to discuss, the idea of saving trees and land and rocks. People say that Hitler was a nature romantic – especially left-wing people who have gone green and want to turn this into a post-colonialism struggle. But that's beside the point. As if a factory worker can't enjoy nature, or a fisherman in Bangladesh. I'm talking now about the fact that we need to teach ourselves to see nature again, to become truly aware of it,' he said with such conviction that Erik felt himself nodding as if hypnotised.

Helena tried to apologise. 'You're totally right, Chris. What I meant is that ...'

But Chris motioned for her to stop, and she immediately fell silent.

Erik suddenly felt that Chris's voice was speaking to him in a way that literally got under his skin. Yet he now came to a realisation that struck him with full force: Chris was actually grieving because he was no longer a child and out hiking with his father. The idea made him shiver, and he felt euphoric as he thought about his own father, who had always been working, who had never been home, and maybe that's what Chris had been talking about all along. Erik hadn't thought about this earlier, but he now realised that he'd had almost no contact with his own father, and that must mean something in the big picture of things.

It was as if Chris were now continuing with this thought as he said: 'You grow up and your happiness is no longer pure. You realise that you also have to let go, you can't stay an idealist your whole life. So, now I think it's time to prepare the bonfire,' he said. Erik felt like applauding.

It was a sculpture made of branches and straw, about three

metres in height, depicting a man. It resembled some strange sort of maypole. Erik had never seen anything like it. He'd thought they were going to gather sticks in the woods and build a traditional bonfire on the beach.

'Did you make this yourself?' he asked Chris.

'With some help from the others. It doesn't take that long if you've done it before. About three hours,' he said.

'So what's going to happen now?'

Roger, Helena and Ville had helped fasten the sculpture, or whatever it was, to a structure made of boards. Then they had placed rocks around it in a circle.

It was still light out, and it would probably stay that way all night. Ylva and Roger had emerged from the house. They had changed clothes and were wearing kimonos. Julia and Marika came back from the sauna. So now everyone was gathered on the beach.

Chris got out what looked like masks made of bark, and he suggested that everyone sit in a circle around the sculpture. Roger began reading aloud from a poem, which he introduced as T. S. Eliot's 'The Hollow Men', translated into Swedish.

When he was finished, Chris lit a joint and passed it around. Ville fetched several drums and slowly started tapping on them. Roger went to the sauna and fetched a big horn, which he began to play. It made a surprisingly low sound, a deep and hypnotic rumbling. Erik took a drag on the joint and passed it on.

They sat like that for at least an hour, until Chris stood up and lit the bonfire. The sculpture didn't flare up immediately. Instead, it slowly began to burn with a timid blue flame that spread inside of the figure. It seemed barbaric for them to be setting fire to a human form, but Erik didn't want to question the symbolism behind the act. Maybe this was also part of obliterating humankind. His body was feeling too relaxed for him to care about trying to interpret everything.

Gradually they all got to their feet, one by one. Chris went down to the water, and the others followed. At the shoreline Chris leaned down and began drawing something in the sand. Ville had brought along one of the drums and began striking it harder as Roger blew on the horn, bumping and grinding his hips, thrusting his pelvis.

Ylva took off her kimono and stepped into the water, where she smeared her body with sand and mud. Now and then Helena made a grunting sound, and Marika responded by barking like a dog. She danced around in a circle while she looked up at the pale sky.

Only now did Erik look at Julia, who seemed as fascinated by the whole scene as he was.

'What the hell are they doing?' asked Julia, sounding drunk.

Erik merely smiled. Much to his surprise, he noticed he had an erection. His dick was pressing against his trousers.

While the others danced on the beach, Julia sat down a short distance away to watch. She'd brought a glass of wine. She asked Erik to sit down with her, but he began laughing uncontrollably and went over to join the dancers.

'Isn't this amazing?' called Marika to Julia as she danced in the water and welcomed Erik to the ritual. He kept on laughing and began copying Chris, writing words with big letters in the sand.

By now Roger and Ylva had completely smeared their bodies with mud and were rubbing against each other. They were visible only as dark silhouettes against the backdrop of the water.

Julia felt drunk and worn out. She could see somebody moving over the rocks some distance away. At first she thought it was one of the children, but then she realised it was a grown-up.

'Who's that over there?' she asked the others.

Chris paused and looked.

'That's our neighbour. I invited her to the party, but she declined,' he said.

'I think she radiates a sad energy,' said Helena.

Chris shouted to the woman.

'Hey there! Would you like to come over and have a glass of wine with us?'

The woman turned around to look at them, then shook her head. She kept walking across the rocks.

Ville was now playing an intense rhythm on the drum, and he started chanting a yoik.

Julia stood up and brushed off the sand.

'Shall we go?' she asked Erik, who was standing on the beach looking at the others.

Erik's head was spinning pleasantly after Julia fell asleep. He'd enjoyed the sex more than usual, as if he were sensing more things all at once, both his own desire and Julia's, as if his consciousness had left his head and seeped into his whole body, all the way out to his fingertips.

First he had sent the children up to the attic, and for once they offered no protest. Alice had seemed tired but happy. Then he and Julia had retreated to the bedroom after getting washed up and brushing their teeth. Erik had looked at himself in the mirror and grimaced. For the first time he noticed there were streaks of grey at his temples.

He could still feel the rush like a loud buzzing in his head. He was wide awake as he lay in bed, facing the window.

The house was wrapped in silence, as if the discussions of the evening had nothing to do with it, as if the house wanted to say that it was too old to care about such matters.

Erik turned over in bed and realised he couldn't sleep. Besides, he was hungry.

He got up and walked barefoot through the house to the kitchen. He opened the fridge, noticing now what Julia had mentioned earlier. There was an odd smell coming from the drain. A damp and slightly sour smell, like old pipes.

The bottle of Bacardi stood on the worktop. He saw that it had been opened. He'd bought it with the romantic notion of having a drink every evening in Mjölkviken, but so far he hadn't felt like it.

He rummaged in the fridge, taking out some cold cuts and butter. He made himself four big sandwiches and greedily ate them all. He could hear his jaws working steadily. The whole process of eating filled his mind. He poured himself a shot of rum.

He stood in the kitchen for a while, looking out of the window at the shadows of Midsummer Eve stretching across the yard. It was so quiet. He was overcome by a feeling that he had a hard time fending off. A feeling that he was useless, replaceable, as if someone else entirely could be standing here holding a glass of rum.

He'd managed to forget all his worries for one evening, but now they came back to him full force.

He would probably find another job. He'd be doing pretty much the same thing no matter where he worked. He'd receive complaints from people and then try to explain as pedagogically as possible how they needed to solve the problem. And once in a while he'd be confronted with unusually difficult problems, but in the end he'd be able to solve those too. And he'd have colleagues he was able to stand, maybe even a few that he liked, and they would all grow older, and eventually it would become apparent to all of them that this was how things had turned out. This was their life.

He went back to the bedroom, got into bed and pulled up the covers as he tried to burrow into the darkness. But he couldn't sleep. The house was breathing quietly, and suddenly he heard that sound coming from the tennis court.

Erik got up again but didn't even put on his shoes. He simply went out the front door and walked straight down to the road, then followed the path to the beach.

It was light outside.

The air was clear and still. A faint rushing came from the sea. He felt sand and pine needles under his feet as he walked.

He slowed down as he approached the tennis court and moved more cautiously so as not to draw attention.

He was practically holding his breath as he went up the short driveway and around the red-painted house that stood at one end of the court.

There was no car in sight, but he could hear someone playing tennis, just like a few days ago.

A small incline made it impossible for him to see what was happening on the tennis court. He took a few more steps forward and could make out a figure, animated and distinct in the clear midsummer night. The ball slammed against the opposite wall.

It was a woman. She had on black sweatpants, a sweatshirt, and a pair of neon-yellow shoes. Her hair was pulled back into a ponytail.

Abruptly she stopped playing. Erik could hear his own breathing. The woman picked up a bottle of water and took a swig. He felt himself glued to the spot. He couldn't stop looking at her. By the time he came to his senses and realised she was bound to see him, it was too late.

Erik backed away. 'Shhh!' he said. 'I mean, I'm sorry! There's no reason to be scared. I mean, I didn't intend to scare you ... I was just out for a walk, and I heard somebody playing ...'

But he'd frightened her. She ran from the tennis court and disappeared into the shadows, carrying the water bottle in one hand and the tennis racket in the other.

5

THE BEDROOM WAS BATHED in light. Julia had forgotten to hang up the sheet over the window, and now she'd been awakened by the sun shining in her face.

When she got up her crotch felt sticky. Slowly memories of the night came back to her – the party, the conversations, the gloomy mood at the beach, the water, the wine.

After the kids had gone to bed in the attic, Julia and Erik had made love, and they'd been much too loud about it. She'd been a little drunk, and Erik seemed to be high. It had taken him a long time to come. Right now he was still lying in bed and didn't even react when she pulled off the covers and wrapped them around her shoulders before going into the kitchen.

A headache started up somewhere in the nerve canals of her brain. Alice was sitting in the kitchen eating breakfast and reading a book. Had she been awake when her parents had sex? If so, had she heard everything? Maybe it didn't matter. Yet Julia thought it was awkward seeing her daughter here in the sunny kitchen when all the sensations of sex still lingered in her body.

They didn't speak to each other. Julia went over to the sink and poured herself a glass of water from the tap. She drank it quickly, followed by two more glasses of water.

She looked out of the window. It was a radiant day.

'Is Anton up?' asked Julia.

'I have no idea,' said Alice.

'I think I'll go back to bed.'

Julia stopped in the bathroom to wash herself and then climbed back into bed. She lay perfectly still, thinking that otherwise she might get sick. She stared up at the ceiling and tried not to make any sudden moves.

Like most people suffering from a hangover, she had a feeling that something embarrassing had happened during the evening. But what could it be? In her mind she went over the first two hours and found nothing to worry about. She thought about how they had all greeted each other, about the dinner they had shared, and about the conversation regarding the climate. It had all been enjoyable and quite harmless.

But then she recalled what was bothering her: Marika. There was something about the whole mood between them, an air of insincerity. She thought now about the way she had talked about Erik, the way she had listened to Marika, nodding at what she said. She'd become the old Julia who never dared contradict her friend. Yet she also thought about her novel. It was a form of betrayal, and Marika had no idea what Julia had written about her. And then she thought about the party on the beach and Erik's strange behaviour, and the sexual energy ... It was all too much, and Julia buried her head in the pillow as if to hide from the world.

Why was she acting like this? Why had she decided to drink? She was supposed to be writing.

She could easily avoid Marika for the rest of the summer if she tried. They'd hardly spent any time talking to each other, maybe an hour or two but no more than that. It was embarrassing to think that somewhere inside she was the same person she used to be as a child, and that Marika could cast the same spell over her. Why did Julia still want to impress the little rich girl who lived nearby? Yet she was also annoyed with the grown-up Marika. Her relationship with Chris seemed like play-acting, a performance.

She could hear Anton coming down from the attic. He came into the room and crawled into bed next to her without saying a word. His movements made her feel a surge of nausea, and she forced herself to lie very still.

'Did you have a nice evening?' she asked.

For a moment he didn't speak.

'Mamma?' he said then.

'Yes, sweetheart?'

'You were gone a long time. I didn't know when you were coming back.'

'I know. I'm sorry. But today we'll do something fun,' she said, giving him a hug. He turned to face her and crept nearer so he was lying very close. If she lay totally still, she could almost forget the pounding headache and the nausea ominously gathering in her stomach. She closed her eyes and stroked Anton's hair. He'd always been incredibly attached to her, and that scared her a bit. But she saw so much of herself in him. He was always talking about the way things tasted and smelled and felt, as if his senses were more acute than most people's. Maybe she could make the world a little gentler for him, not as cruel. She'd been the same way as a child, just as overwhelmed by the world, just as aware of her own sensory impressions and emotions.

'Mamma?' he said again.

She opened her eyes.

'Yes?'

'Do you like being a mother?'

She turned her head to peer at him. He was staring at her with such earnestness. His eyes were exactly the same green as her own.

'Of course I do. Why do you ask?'

'Because of something Leo said.'

'What did he say?'

'That his father didn't want to be grown up.'

'Oh, sweetie. I love being your mother,' she said, kissing the top of his head. The nausea was getting worse. It was so bad now that she needed to dash for the bathroom.

'Sorry, but I have to go to the toilet,' she said, climbing over him and running out of the bedroom. She threw up into the toilet bowl, dark red vomit with pieces from yesterday's dinner. At least she'd made it to the bathroom in time, but her nostrils had filled with scraps of bulgur and bits of parsley. She blew her nose on a tissue and drank water directly from the tap. Then she rinsed her face. She instantly felt better, even though she'd broken out in a cold sweat, and she was ashamed to leave the bathroom and have to meet Alice in the kitchen.

Eventually Erik also awoke. He came into the kitchen and seemed to be in a good mood. He made himself three big sandwiches and then sat down on the steps to eat them. Alice was lying on the rocks, peering dreamily at the tarn as she listened to music. Anton had fetched the little wooden house from the terrace and was busy filling it with tiny twigs he had cut from pine branches.

'So did you have fun with Alice and that boy yesterday?' Julia asked him.

She'd made herself a small omelette. Her appetite had returned after she'd thrown up.

'Leo taught us a new card game. Could we play it later?'

Erik went into the cellar to have a look at the pipes. Maybe he'd forgotten about the strange rituals on the beach because he'd seemed totally unconcerned and happy all morning, like a well-rested person who was ready for new adventures.

'I don't know whether I dare mess with the pipes, but I'll check to see how things look down there,' he'd said.

Julia nodded.

'What else did you do yesterday?' she asked Alice, who hadn't been listening. She was staring at her mobile.

'Alice? I'm talking to you.'

'What?!' said Alice, looking up with annoyance.

'I asked you what else you did yesterday.'

Alice gave her mother a distracted look. Then she took her headphones out.

'Leo kissed Alice,' said Anton without looking up.

Julia gave him an amused look.

'He did?'

'It wasn't a tongue kiss, but it was still a kiss. On the mouth.'

Julia glanced at her daughter, who was lying on the ground. Alice had apparently become a teenager.

'Let's not talk any more about that right now,' Julia whispered to Anton, who nodded. Yet she felt herself blushing as she thought about her own evening, as if what Alice had done was analogous to what she'd done, as if they were all now entangled with that strange family on the other side of the road.

Julia couldn't imagine sitting down to write today, not in her present condition, yet she felt a strong urge to get back to her novel. There was something about what happened yesterday that made her feel a need to immerse herself in the story. All the small occurrences of daily life often had that effect on her. She'd get a feeling that she was glimpsing a part of life that existed beyond what was rational and explicable, something that touched on primal urges, something that eluded her if she tried to analyse it.

Erik emerged from the cellar and got himself a cup of coffee. His hair was dishevelled, which Julia found endearing. He was unshaven and emanated a certain vigour, which was a blend of muscles and a sense that he was comfortable with his body. He'd always managed to look good the 'day after'.

'Shall we go for a walk in the woods?' he asked. 'We can have a look at the moose. You kids will have to show us where it is.'

The whole family headed for the woods, as if on an expedition.

'It's over there,' said Anton, who was leading the way.

Julia wasn't really prepared for how big the animal was. It looked as if it had been there a very long time because the body was more or less dried out and gnawed, with parts of the skeleton clearly visible. Only the moose's legs and hooves seemed to have been spared, and there were still some patches of fur remaining. Its entrails had been completely hollowed out, but the head, or rather the skull, was eerily expressive, as if the moose were looking right at them. It was like a spooky cubist painting.

'Do you think we should phone somebody?' asked Erik.

He seemed more fascinated than horrified.

'That's probably a good idea. The corpse will attract a lot of bacteria now that it's summer. Plus, I think you're supposed to report things like this,' said Julia. 'I wonder how long it's been here.'

'Pappa, why is it hanging in the tree?' asked Anton.

Julia also thought that was strange. How had it ended up like that? It was hanging a good half metre above the ground, if not more.

'I think it must have got stuck during the winter and froze to death. Then it thawed out in the springtime. The snow was probably very deep around here, but then the snow melted. That must be what happened. It must have fought hard. It's a big animal, after all. It seems strange that the moose couldn't manage to get free,' said Erik.

Julia felt a lump form in her throat as she gazed at the moose. The nausea returned, and it wasn't just because of how the animal looked. It was also at the thought of the moose standing here for days, maybe weeks, without food or any way to rest. Fighting a fierce battle to the death. Maybe it had caused a huge ruckus, but no one had heard it high up here in the woods in the middle of winter. Maybe the moose had eventually given up and let the cold take over, deciding not to struggle any more. Moose were big animals, and it seemed likely they were intelligent enough to fear death.

They stood in silence around the moose. Anton took Julia's hand. Erik walked around it again, squatting down to take a closer look at the corpse. Then they headed back to the house in silence, walking in single file.

A hunter from the area came over in the afternoon to help Erik haul away the moose. The hunter had a grey beard, and he wore a green jacket. He shook hands with Erik and gave his name, speaking in a muffled voice. The two of them cleared everything away. They threw all the parts of the cadaver in black rubbish sacks, which the hunter then stowed in his big van while Julia stood in the yard and watched.

Later in the afternoon it started to rain. Julia felt like going for a swim, but the kids didn't want to go along. Erik suggested they take a sauna first.

'A Midsummer Day sauna. Doesn't that sound like a good idea?' he said.

He was right. They sat in the sauna for a long time, sweating out the effects of the night. Julia soon felt like a new person. She and Erik put on their dressing gowns and walked barefoot down to the shore. Pine needles and sand and stones prickled the soles of their feet, but it also felt both lovely and real. The rain didn't bother them; it actually warmed up the water. Julia tossed her dressing gown on the rocks near the bay and waded out as far as she could go. She caught a faint whiff of rotting fish, the sort of smell that comes from seagulls. The wind was blowing in from the sea, and raindrops lashed at her face.

Erik came into the water and swam over to her. Then he

swam further out, taking strong crawl strokes, before he turned around and came back to her. It wasn't deep where she was standing. The water reached only to her waist. She would have to swim almost out of the bay before the water got so deep she couldn't touch bottom.

'Oh, this is great,' said Erik. 'It might be the greatest thing there is. I mean it,' he said.

'I know,' said Julia.

'Did you have fun yesterday?' he asked.

He swam over to her and touched her waist. She let her body fall backwards so the water covered her neck. He came closer and gently grabbed her left breast.

'Did you have fun?' she asked.

'Yes. It was a little … different,' said Erik. 'Is she the one you wrote about?'

'Who do you mean?'

'Marika. In your book.'

'I suppose she was the model. But it's fiction, you know. We were childhood friends, and a person's memory isn't always reliable. I made up most of it. We spent maybe three or four summers here. Our parents knew each other.'

'It's strange that you hardly ever talk about this place, and that we haven't stayed here before. It's perfect for us.'

'It's like this place exists more in my body than in my brain. And I think I exhausted the topic when I wrote my novel.'

He let her go and slid back into the water.

'Do you ever think about what all of them were discussing last night?' he asked her. 'About the environment?'

'What do you mean?'

'I mean, do you really think that could happen? That the world will end or humankind will be obliterated? If we're to believe what those people were saying, there's no longer any hope for us.'

'Sometimes,' said Julia. 'Sometimes I think about that.'

'I think it's horrible to keep imagining that disaster is waiting just around the corner. I wonder what that does to us, to human beings in general. Are we in a perpetual state of crisis?'

Julia didn't reply as she floated in the water.

He went over to her, shivering in the rain. 'I think I'll go in. Coming?'

'Maybe in a while.'

She was cold, but she didn't want to get out of the water yet. She felt like staying in this setting, in the moment. She swam a little further out, then dived under as she thought about a short story by John Cheever that she'd always liked. It was about a man who decides to take a detour home by swimming in all the neighbour's pools, going from one yard to the next. Along the way, some of the neighbours offer him drinks. They're having a barbecue, and eventually the mood gets stranger and stranger, while the seasons of the year change.

She thought about how swimming was like booze and how you disappeared down into the depths, yet water was also associated with purification.

Erik stood on the shore, using a towel to dry off. She ought to get out and go home with him, but instead she turned around and kept on swimming as she glanced up at the beach and the big grey house.

When she headed back to the summer house, she found Erik in the sauna. He had lit a candle. His skin was almost burning to the touch when she sat down next to him.

'How was it?' he asked.

'Great,' she replied.

Neither of them spoke for quite a while. Julia was thinking she ought to be talking, but she refrained because she didn't know what to say.

Erik stroked her cheek.

'Do you think ...' he began. 'I mean ... doesn't it feel like things have gone a bit stale between us lately?'

She felt a lump form in her stomach. 'Maybe you're right,' she said, pulling her legs up to rest her chin on her knees.

'How's the writing coming along?' he asked.

'It's okay.'

She couldn't find the right words. She tried to think of what else to say. Then she happened to think of the children.

'Anton is so sweet.'

'He sure is. He seems to be thriving out here.'

'He told me something strange today.'

'What did he say?'

'Something about how Leo's father can't act like a grown-up. I wonder what he meant.'

'Chris? He seems very grown up to me. And very confident about his cause.'

'But in a way, Anton could be right,' said Julia. 'There actually aren't any rules any more about how to be a grown-up.'

'What do you mean?'

She sat up straight and threw more water on the sauna stones. Steam instantly rose up to the ceiling.

'I mean, there's no ideal way to act. Our own parents rebelled against a conservative generation. They listened to rock music, and certain people – like Ylva and Roger from yesterday – have tried to work out an alternative lifestyle, with open relationships, and that sort of thing ... But our generation doesn't believe in that kind of solution. So we live a super bourgeois life, almost as if we've gone back to the 1950s.'

'We haven't really, have we?' said Erik.

'In some ways, yes. Just think about it. Marriage has won a new status. It's once again considered desirable. Yet we're not really satisfied with marriage. We want to be free and leave all doors open. We want the children to give meaning to our life, yet we also want to live egotistically,' said Julia.

'I have no need to leave all doors open,' said Erik.

'That's not what I'm saying,' replied Julia. 'It's just that sometimes I think it's stupid there aren't other models for how to be a grown-up and live together other than the nuclear family unit.'

She could hear how that sounded, as if she were using politics as a means for talking about her own feelings and insecurities.

'Are you talking about your writing now?'

They'd had this discussion often, occasionally even quarrelling over it. The fact that she needed solitude and isolation in order to write. But this time it was different. This was about her longing for something that would change her sense of loneliness.

'No, that's not what I mean. Well, maybe. I'm not sure. Sometimes I think I'd like to have a … mature relationship. Sort of like Marika and Chris. A relationship that's not based on meeting at the age of twenty and then staying together because that's the only sensible thing to do. Just because … You know, we've been together a really long time, and I think everyone changes, as a person. Oh, I don't know.'

Erik scratched his leg. He seemed amused. She could feel the sweat running down her forehead. She was annoyed that he wasn't taking her seriously.

'So you want to be like Marika and Chris? And live in a collective?' he asked.

'Good God, no.'

'I know you. And you need me.'

Now she got angry, maybe mostly because he was right. He did know her. At the same time, he couldn't know what it felt like to be her, to feel the way she did. He couldn't fix things or take away her loneliness. The only thing he could do was to pronounce a diagnosis and then judge her and think she was a hopeless human being.

And maybe she really was a hopeless human being. Or maybe it was very simple: they had grown apart.

'You don't understand,' she said.

'In what way?'

'I mean … Maybe I don't understand either.'

'Huh,' said Erik.

They sat in silence for a while. Julia threw more water on the stones. She felt like she could talk to Erik, and yet she couldn't. If she really tried to tell him how she felt, she would end up hurting him.

'So when are your parents getting here?' he asked.

'I don't think they'll come over until Alice's birthday.'

'They always seem to have a lot of things planned.'

'Uh-huh. They have both the time and the money,' said Julia.

'Is everything okay with them?'

'I have no idea. My mother is never satisfied with anything,' she said.

At that instant it occurred to her that she was the same way.

'Oh my God.'

'What?'

'Nothing. Or rather, I was just thinking that I'm a lot like my mother. Nothing is ever good enough. Everything is a disaster. I'm her daughter, after all. Why should I be any different?'

'But you don't have to be like her. You can do something about it. You are satisfied sometimes, aren't you?' Erik asked.

'Sure. Of course. Once in a while,' said Julia.

She leaned back against the hot wall.

'Sorry,' she said. 'But you were the one who wanted to talk about us.'

'I just wanted to have a normal discussion. I thought we could try to talk about our relationship.'

Julia threw more water on the stones. A big scoopful, this time. Steam rose up towards them like a wall. Both of them had to hunch over, pressing their chests to their knees.

Erik stood up abruptly.

'I think I'll go rinse off. See you back at the house.'

6

That's what happened when the solar system closed
its vaulted gate of the purest crystal
and separated the people of the spaceship Aniara
from all the connections and promises of the sun

And abandoned to terror-hardened space
we dispersed our call of Aniara
through clear-as-glass infinity, but achieved nothing.

Excerpt from *Aniara* by Harry Martinson

MANIFESTO FOR A WORLD IN MOURNING

All grief begins with denial, a refusal to accept the loss. That's
where many of us now find ourselves. With the last of our
strength we cling tightly to the hope that maybe, just maybe,
we will awake from this nightmare, shake off the anxieties of
the night, and step forward into a morning that is exactly like
all previous mornings.

But ultimately, the flames of hope are extinguished, and
what's left is only empty space and a bewildered human with
no map, with no possibility of finding his bearings in the dark.

We who prioritise the Movement, Aniara, believe that there

is also power in powerlessness, that the new tomorrow can be beautiful only when we accept our loss and our eyes grow accustomed to the dark. When we give up any thoughts of saving ourselves and our conscience by means of solar panels and recycling, through technological solutions and a smarter capitalism.

Now is the time to face the truth: it's too late.

Now is the time to listen to the sound of the funeral dirge; it's tolling loud and clear and has been for a long time. It's tolling for a nature that never had a chance to defend itself; it's tolling for the silent beauty that no one cares about, for the tiny defenceless bugs in the ground, for the birds in the sky, for all that we never saw.

Now the leaves are falling. As Edith Södergran wrote: we ought to 'love life's long hours of illness'; we should no longer close our eyes.

There are far too many of us who have grown weary of keeping alive the ever fainter flame, who have done so much for so many years although nothing got any better. Now is the time to mourn. Only then can we go on.

Aniara is not about hope. It's about a belief that there is still beauty to be discovered; that there are small, beautiful pockets in the world from which we can draw sustenance. It's about pushing aside everything we've learned about the good forces of civilisation. Right vs left, socialism vs capitalism – they can be contained in a single word: narcissism. It's the same narcissism that makes us search for an endless stream of impressions, that makes us need constant kicks so as not to become apathetic. It's the vast, numbing feeling that has struck all of us, that sets in after several hours spent in front of our glaring screens, the constant hunt for something, as we are promised WE WON'T BELIEVE WHAT HAPPENS NEXT.

We say: put away your phones, smash your screens. Because THIS is what will happen next: an unknown future in which the only thing left is the tiny grain of sand on the glowing, blood-red shore. Learn to see in the dark; learn to move with the aid of all your senses; discover new senses. Rebel against 'the great absurdity of living' (Harry Martinson). Rebel against the attempt to 'reach a crevice / that allows in a glimpse of the glow of hope'. Forget hope. Say yes to despair.

Chris Blackwood
The Aniara Movement

7

EARLY ON A WARM JULY morning, as Erik was taking a walk, he met the woman from the tennis court. She was standing next to a slightly rusty, green woman's bike, trying to fix the chain. When she was finished and got on the bike, he noticed that the chain was still loose and would most likely come off again.

'You should tighten that,' he said.

Erik had been going down the beach more often, having a vague feeling that he was searching for something. He would glance at the tennis court, but he hadn't caught sight of the woman. He would leave Julia sitting on the terrace, working on her book. She seemed very focused, and the discussions of the past few days hadn't led anywhere. Instead, they were hardly speaking to each other. He felt inspired to do something new, to make a real effort, but she seemed tired and unreachable, as if she didn't want to let him get closer.

The woman was tall and slender, almost as tall as Erik, and maybe about forty-five or so. She was wearing dark jeans and a man's checked shirt with the sleeves rolled up. When she turned to look at him, her expression was impassive and impossible to decipher, neither friendly nor hostile.

'Does it come off a lot? The chain?' he said.

'It comes off every time I want to go somewhere,' she said. 'I suppose I ought to do something about it.'

'I'm Erik,' he said, offering to shake her hand.

'Kati,' she said.

Her voice was a bit raspy and muted, as if issuing from an old transistor radio.

'I'm sorry that I interrupted your tennis game. Do you often play in the middle of the night?'

She didn't answer as she fixed her eyes on her bicycle.

'You just need to pull the wheel backwards a little, and that will tighten the chain. You don't have a car?'

'I don't have a driver's license. But I usually get by with a bike,' she said.

He thought to himself that she was the sort of person who was used to attracting attention from men and having most things taken care of for her. She had that kind of look; she was beautiful, with high cheekbones. So what was she doing here alone?

'Shall I have a look?'

It was an older-model Crescent bicycle, probably from the seventies. He remembered seeing a similar bike from his childhood, although it was a different colour.

'Do you have an adjustable wrench?'

He grabbed the handlebars, pretending to inspect the bike.

'Do you think that's necessary?' she asked.

'I could tighten the chain.'

'There should be some tools in the shed,' she said.

'I have a wrench at home if you don't have one.'

'I think I do. Shall I fetch it?'

'I'll come with you.'

They walked down to the shore, to the big house that stood in the centre of the curving shoreline. Erik followed her to a small shed behind the house. The woman didn't say a word as she stepped forward to unlock the shed and then stepped inside. It was filled with junk: cushions for patio furniture, a heat lamp, a surfboard, water skis, cross-country skis. Things belonging to a family, thought Erik. That seemed strange because he hadn't pictured her with a family.

She spent a while searching, and in the meantime he tried not to stare at her, merely casting brief glances at her back as he smiled and tried to look as if he was waiting politely. Finally she found a toolbox in a corner. They took it with them back to the road.

She stood next to him without speaking as he turned the bike upside down and pulled the rear wheel no more than a centimetre back.

'All right. Now the chain shouldn't come off as often,' he said.

She smiled.

'That's great. I don't know why I didn't do that earlier.'

'Just let me know if there's anything else I can help with.'

She gave him another smile, standing next to the bike, as if she was waiting for him to leave before she could cycle away.

'Thanks,' she said.

'No problem,' said Erik. 'I'm just on my way down to the beach.'

The remark sounded stupid, since it was obvious that's where he was going.

He'd been so immersed in the strange mood that he'd forgotten he was still holding her wrench. He didn't notice until she cycled off, and he reached the water's edge. He went back and set it on the steps of her house, and then couldn't resist peering in a window. It was dark inside, and it looked much the same as any other house, yet something didn't seem right. The dining table was cluttered, and there were dirty cups scattered about the room.

He stood on the shore and gazed at the horizon, but he could no longer remember why he'd come down here.

When he went back up to the summer house, Alice was lying on a mattress that she'd dragged onto the ground. She was staring at her phone. Anton was sitting on a big rock at the tarn, holding a fishing rod.

'Caught anything?' asked Erik.

'I'm mostly catching water lilies,' he replied with a shrug. 'But Mamma says there are fish here. And sometimes I've seen them jumping in the water.'

'How'd you like to get a real casting rod so you can try catching fish in the sea? We could buy one the next time we go into town.'

Anton looked at him, seeming to consider changing rods, but then he raised his eyebrows to show it didn't make any difference to him. Erik could understand that. Sometimes there was a certain comfort about fishing at a hopeless place, where you didn't need to worry about catching anything.

Julia was sitting on the terrace, working on her laptop. Erik still hadn't told her about being sacked from his job, and by now he didn't feel as if he would.

'How's it going?' he asked.

She didn't look up, keeping her eyes focused on the computer screen. Erik felt slightly relieved that he didn't have to think about her, since she was so clearly immersed in her work. He had asked how it was going merely to be nice, but if she didn't answer, that meant he needn't be concerned. Instead, he lost himself in thoughts about Kati, wondering who she was, why she was living down on the shore alone, and who owned all those things in the shed.

Julia closed the lid of her laptop.

'Did you ask me something?'

Her hair was pulled back in a ponytail. She looked worried.

'How's it going?' he asked again.

'Okay,' she said. 'Well, I'm not really sure. I can never plan anything. I just write and write and hope the story will come together and start living its own life. But I think I have the characters worked out now. I think I know who they are.'

'Well, that's at least something,' he said.

'What have you been doing today?' she asked.

'Nothing special.'

'Are you bored?'

'What do you mean?'

'Because you're not at work. Is there anything for you to do here? Maybe you should go and have a talk with Chris. Or go back down into the cellar and fix the pipes.'

'Hmm … I don't know. Maybe. I don't really know anything about fixing pipes,' replied Erik. Julia's parents would be arriving in a couple of days, which seemed like bad timing to Erik. He had no desire to see them, considering how things were at the moment.

'I went down to the beach today. You know that woman who lives there?'

'In that house? The woman who's so cross?'

'I don't know whether she's cross.'

'They said she radiates negative energy. Did you talk to her?'

Erik felt himself blushing.

'I helped her fix the chain on her bicycle. It had hopped off.'

'Ah. What's her name?'

'Kati, I think.'

'Does she speak Finnish?'

'I think so,' he replied.

For a moment neither of them spoke. Julia picked up her manuscript from the table and leafed through it distractedly.

'I think she has a family,' he said.

She looked up from the manuscript.

'She does?'

He didn't feel like explaining.

The next day he went down to the beach again to take a walk. He'd talked to Chris in the morning because they'd run into each other by accident. Erik had only vague and confused memories of the beach party. He recalled only the gentle warmth around the bonfire, and he thought maybe he should be embarrassed about having lost control, but he didn't feel like being embarrassed.

He was on his way back when he saw Kati walking her bike down the path towards her house. She propped the bike against the shed in the yard.

'Is it working okay now?' he asked.

'It's great. Thanks a lot,' she said.

'It was nothing. Just let me know if you need help with anything else.'

She picked up two grocery bags. He rushed over to carry them for her.

'Thanks,' she said.

'Are you going to be here all summer?' asked Erik.

'Why do you ask?'

'Oh, no reason. I was just wondering whether you have a long holiday.'

'I'll probably stay all summer,' she said. 'At least until September.'

He walked with her up to the terrace and set the grocery bags next to the door. He wanted to keep talking but didn't know what to say. He suddenly felt so stupid.

'I'm off all summer too,' he said.

'Are you?' she said.

'Yes. In fact ...'

He paused for a moment but then decided to say it.

'I've been sacked from my job. So I'll have to look for another one in the autumn.'

'That's too bad,' she said.

Erik felt as if he wanted to tell her something personal, confide in her.

'Yes, I suppose it is. But I'm sure things will work out. I haven't told anyone yet. I haven't told my wife, I mean.'

She gave him an odd look. That was the wrong thing to say.

'Sometimes it's easier to talk to other people,' he said.

'I suppose so,' she said.

For the rest of the afternoon Erik had a feeling that everything was going smoothly. When he drove to the supermarket to buy salmon, when he cooked dinner out in the yard, the warmth he felt for his children as the family ate together, and even when he had a phone call from his brother later in the evening.

Anders was in Vietnam and wanted to borrow money to buy a plane ticket back to Finland.

'And I wonder if I could stay with you guys for a while, just until I find a place of my own.'

'But we're in Mjölkviken right now. Were you thinking of coming out here?' asked Erik.

'Do you have room?'

Erik thought he should ask Julia first, but considering how she'd been acting lately, he couldn't bring himself to do that.

'There's plenty of sleeping space up in the attic. Have you had a good trip?'

'I'll tell you about it later.'

8

ANDERS NOTICED THE COOL summer air of
Finland as soon as he stepped out of the airplane in Vanda. The
air was drier than in Asia, the airport was emptier, everything
was quieter, and he felt unpleasantly foreign and grubby as he
walked through the clean and Nordically gleaming terminal,
heading for the exit. While he waited for his suitcases among
the weary Finnish families with young children, he had a feeling
that he was returning to Finland after several years, even though
he'd been away only three months.

The trip had not gone as he'd hoped. He'd spent all his
money and suffered a breakdown one night after an evening of
heavy drinking. He woke up on the bank of a river, surrounded
by street vendors and staring tourists. He didn't really know
why he'd decided to go to Hanoi, but he realised the trip hadn't
had the positive effect he'd wanted. He felt defeated, like an
example in some self-help book seeking to illustrate its moral:
Don't run away from your problems by creating geographical
distance. Instead you should always first try to work things out
for yourself.

Why had he decided to make the trip at all? Anders had been
dreaming about it for a long time, yearning to be swallowed
up by the Asian heat and feverish activity. He'd known nothing
about Hanoi other than what he'd read on the internet, but he
did have some idea what to expect: a city with a vibrant pulse

and, above all, a totally anonymous place where he would be far away from his family.

During the first weeks he had walked around aimlessly, looking at the street vendors and their big piles of frogs, at all the chickens that seemed to be running around loose. He walked down alleyways and stared right into people's living rooms, at the blaring TV sets and children clinging to their mother's skirts.

He'd taken lodging at a hostel for backpackers, thinking it might be a positive way to start off his trip. Anders hadn't bought a return plane ticket. Instead, he'd dreamed of travelling back to Finland by train, maybe via China and the trans-Siberian railway, but that was a plan he'd put off thinking about until later. His travel funds consisted of two thousand euros, money he'd mostly borrowed, and in his suitcase he'd packed a bunch of books: novels by Thomas Bernhard; Freud's case studies; a few guidebooks about Vietnam; and *Sönder*, a novel by the Finland-Swedish writer Henry Parland. Anders had read the book at least ten times, finding in it his own general feeling of rootlessness in life. The novel, from 1930, had a splintered storyline that seemed to reflect life and his own mental landscape. A miscellany of fragmented experiences, nothing concrete that he could ever seize hold of. And that had also become his life's motto – an acceptance of the splintered structure, instead of believing there was any such thing as a true core.

The area where he was staying had a pleasant urban feel to it, almost as if he were in Barcelona, because just like in Barcelona, the streets were filled with motor scooters. His room was on the third floor, with a shared shower down the hall.

He went out and tried to get his bearings in the city, but each morning he would wake up in the same small room with a feeling that he might as well have stayed home in Finland. He rented a motor scooter and rode merrily through the streets, and for a while it was fun, but eventually he tired of that too.

He went to pubs where he sometimes met other Europeans and went along to their after-parties. Sometimes he talked to women, but he rarely felt happy. He had not magically become different, even though he was on the other side of the world.

Three months later, when he awoke on the riverbank with an excruciating headache, he was forced to phone his brother and ask for money to buy a plane ticket home. He was ashamed to do that, but he was perhaps even more ashamed that he felt homesick.

He'd had nothing to eat except some crisps on the plane, though he'd drunk three tiny bottles of red wine. When he got to the train station in Helsinki, he had to rush for the toilet. The smell that spread was far from pleasant, but it was normal for him to have digestive problems. It was something he'd suffered from all his life.

As he washed his hands, he thought about the dream he'd had on the plane. He dreamt about his family, that they were all home for the Christmas holidays, including Julia and Erik and their kids, and they were watching family videos together. But something happened. Everybody got upset, and the last thing he recalled from the dream was an image of himself racing barefoot through the snow in Ekenäs, along the train tracks. He could still feel the chill inside his body when he awoke in the darkness of the plane.

He was shocked by the sight of his face in the mirror. He looked worn out and bloated. It was not an attractive face. It might have been all right, if he wasn't so big, but he was at least thirty kilos overweight. He'd pictured losing weight while in Vietnam, but instead he'd tried to make himself feel better by eating too much, while he also smoked and drank. He'd put on at least five kilos.

The clear, bright July sun in Finland seemed to be jeering at him, as if it had expected him to come back, only to show him that he was the same, miserable person he was when he left.

The next day Erik was waiting for him at the small train station in Bennäs. It was the first week of July.

'Did you come via Ekenäs? Did you stop to see Mamma and Pappa?' asked Erik.

Anders paused before replying. He was exhausted and hungry, and he hadn't yet had the energy nor the desire to phone his parents.

'I haven't talked to them,' he said then. His brother was always reminding him that there were people who lived carefully planned and humdrum lives, who kept in regular contact with relatives, and who were able to carry on casual conversations. In a way, he admired all that, although Erik's evasive looks told him that all was not as it should be. His brother seemed nervous. He was drumming his fingers on the steering wheel as he drove.

'How long are you staying?' asked Erik.

'Not sure yet,' said Anders. He knew that he needed a lot of sleep, and he'd thought he might be able to do that here in Mjölkviken. Anders had always liked Julia. They got along well together, and Erik's kids were nice. He needed peace and quiet, and maybe a few weeks in which to ponder what he was going to do with the rest of his life.

'How have you been?' asked Erik.

'It was great,' he lied.

'Because you look a little … tired.'

'It's just because I haven't eaten anything. And I haven't slept well. Jet lag, you know. How about you?'

Erik didn't reply.

Anders didn't have much contact with his family. That was also why, strangely enough, it had taken him so long to make the decision to go to Hanoi. He'd wanted to travel as long as he could remember, but something had been holding him back. It was only lately that he'd begun to understand what that was: he was too dependent. If he'd gone to see a shrink – which would have been unthinkable in Ekenäs – he presumably would have uncovered long ago the root of many of his idiosyncrasies. But it had taken him ages to come to that insight on his own.

When Anders was seven, he developed gastrointestinal problems. As an adult, he'd read his own medical records from that time. The doctor had noted that a 'pale young lad came in' or something like that. When he'd started in first grade he'd suddenly begun to lose weight. He suffered from stomach aches, but didn't tell his parents until it became impossible for him to digest his food. He no longer recalled all the details, but he'd ended up having to see the doctor frequently, with two or three years of constant tests, sometimes under sedation, sometimes not. And occasionally he had to travel somewhere, for instance to the hospital in Tammerfors. The whole time his mother kept a watchful eye on him. He was forced to drink great quantities of fluids in order to empty his intestines each time an endoscopy was performed, and he found the prep procedure both difficult and torturous. He could still recall the taste of the saline solution mixed with raspberry juice. After a couple of years of frequent visits to the hospital, he was finally given a diagnosis: Crohn's disease.

'It's beautiful here,' Anders said now as they drove along a wooded track, heading for the summer house where Julia and Erik were staying.

'It is, isn't it? Some of these houses sell for close to half a million euros,' said Erik. 'But it also seems a little run-down. As if the area had its heyday thirty years ago. These days it's practically deserted. There's just a bunch of hippies living in one of the houses near the beach. You might like them.'

As they drove into the yard and parked in front of the summer house, Anders saw his niece and nephew. He realised then that he hadn't brought them any presents. Anton and Alice greeted him and seemed to be watching his every move as he set his suitcases on the terrace. Anders thought maybe it was good for them to see someone different, to see a grown-up who didn't fit the norm of perfection, someone who wasn't doing all that well. He scratched his beard and patted Anton on the head.

The house was nice, if a bit strange. Anders took note of the odd assortment of furniture and the overriding use of pine everywhere: on all the floors and walls.

'We might have to do some remodelling one day if we take over the place,' said Julia. 'But now let's eat.'

The potato salad was a creamy yellow colour, with capers and onion. Anders helped himself to three servings. He realised how much he'd missed Nordic food, and how much better it made him feel to eat a home-cooked meal instead of all the processed fat he'd consumed during his trip.

'That was great,' he said now, looking at Julia. It felt easier to look at her instead of Erik.

'Sometimes I think I'd have a much healthier view of life if only I ate good food like this every day,' he said.

'So why don't you?' asked Erik.

'I always make things too complicated. My plans get to be too big. Then I spend four hours in the kitchen,' said Anders, setting his knife and fork on his plate.

'I don't think cooking is easy,' said Julia. 'But when you have a family, you're forced to learn. The hardest part is coming up with new things to cook every day.'

'Hard for me, you mean,' said Erik. 'Since I'm the one who does all the cooking.'

Anders had noticed it the minute he came inside. There was an oddly persistent tension between Julia and Erik.

'So tell us what you've been doing,' said Julia.

'Nothing special. I rode around on a motorbike, went to pubs, and met a few people,' replied Anders. He had propped his elbows on the table, resting his chin on his hands. When he looked around, it seemed absurd to be sitting here in the midst of the serene Finnish nature.

'Did you have any plans? Anything special you wanted to do?' asked Julia.

'Not really. Well, actually, I wanted to do some reading and eat Vietnamese street food. But otherwise, nothing specific.'

'What are you going to do now?' asked Erik.

In reality, that was the question that everyone, friends and family, had been asking Anders for the past ten years. He felt annoyed because he knew that soon he'd be forced to decide. He could picture himself through their eyes now, but he pushed the image away.

'Maybe I should become a chef. That's what I've always wanted to do.'

After dinner, Anders excused himself and walked down to the beach alone. He strolled along the water's edge, past several summer houses, to a spot where big waves slammed against the rock walls.

The sea looked unbelievably massive compared with the brightly coloured crowds in Hanoi. He took out the packet he was carrying in his pocket. Maybe he should fling the pills into the sea, but that seemed stupid after sending them by post all the way to Finland.

9

A COUPLE OF DAYS LATER Erik and Alice stood by the road waiting for Julia's parents to arrive.

It was easy to miss the narrow drive up to the summer house, so they had positioned themselves at the road to form a welcome committee. Heavy clouds still lingered in the sky after a light rain in the morning. But it was warmer, and Erik had decided they would eat outside.

Now he saw his father-in-law's car come driving through the wooded glade, a brand-new white Volvo with all the latest gadgets. Göran had bought it in the spring and taken Erik for a drive to show him all the bells and whistles. ('Although I haven't shown all of them to Susanne because then she'd forget that you also have to steer the car.')

Alice walked alongside her father as the car turned onto the drive.

'Hi, darling. And happy birthday!' said Susanne as she opened the passenger-side door and got out to give Alice a hug.

'It looks like we're in for some nice weather,' Erik said to his father-in-law.

'That's what I heard on the news. I wasn't expecting that, considering the kind of summer we've had so far.'

'Well, you've managed to make the place look presentable,' said Susanne as she walked up to the house and greeted Julia.

'But the grass needs mowing. And why have you brought that old chair out here?'

She pointed at a rickety chair that Erik had found next to the woodpile.

'Mamma, we haven't really had time to do much. I'm working on my book, and Erik has been looking after the kids.'

'I've always hated that chair. Your father loved it,' said Susanne.

Erik could see how Julia was steeling herself as she put on her best smile and kissed her mother on both cheeks.

'Have you met my brother?' asked Erik.

Anders, who had been sitting on the terrace, came down to say hello.

'Yes, we've met. At the wedding, and I think one other time. Erik told us you've been in Vietnam,' said Göran.

'That's right.'

'I've heard that a lot of partying and drinking goes on there,' said Göran.

'I suppose. To a certain extent,' replied Anders.

'Mamma and Pappa, do you need help with anything?' Julia asked.

Anton had been waiting all day for his grandmother to arrive, but now that she was here, he didn't want to go down to see her because he didn't want to seem too eager. She always brought him a present. Once she gave him an entire Lego police station. He felt a little too old for such things now, and would prefer a new pair of shoes or a computer game, but that was probably expecting too much.

He was sitting on the terrace when she came up the steps to give him a hug.

'So, here's my honey bunch. How are you doing, Anton?'

Anton breathed in his grandmother's sweet and slightly

tangy scent and felt her soft bosom as she pulled him close. As she hugged him, he cast a surreptitious glance at the bags she was holding.

His cheeks felt warm as she released him.

'I've brought presents, but first I have to unpack so I can find them,' she said, setting everything down on the stone floor of the terrace. Anton could have told her exactly where to find the presents because he could see the big plastic bag she was holding in her left hand, but he knew it would be impolite to mention it. Instead, he stood up to greet his grandfather. Anton loved getting hugs.

'So what sort of people are staying at the neighbouring summer house? They looked interesting,' said Göran.

'Where was that?' asked Erik.

'On our way here we saw a skinny guy walking along the road, heading for the Segerkvists' old villa. He had dreadlocks. When we got closer, we saw there seemed to be a bunch of people at the house, and there was a sign too, as if it were some sort of campsite. Just think what the Segerkvists would say if they knew.'

Julia's mother gave her husband a look.

'I mean, they were always so meticulous about their property,' said Göran.

'We've met them,' said Julia. 'Erik and I. The man you mentioned is named Ville. They're getting ready for the apocalypse.'

'The apocalypse?' said Susanne.

'Yes, but it's not that simple. It has to do with the environment. They want to go back to some pre-industrial time,' Julia went on.

'They have a blog,' said Erik.

'I may be wrong, but I don't think blogs existed in the pre-industrial era,' said Anders.

'I think I'll go in and start fixing dinner. Pappa, now that you're here, could you and Erik have a look at the pipes under the house? There's been a strange smell in the kitchen all summer.'

Göran gave her the evasive look she'd seen so many times lately. Her father was sixty-five years old, and he seemed to have decided that he wanted to be left in peace for the rest of his life.

'Believe me, I've tried to fix that sort of thing thousands of times before. It has to do with the land the house is sitting on. Something to do with the way the ground water flows. You're just going to have to live with it,' he said now. Julia thought it sounded as if he were talking about his marriage.

'I'll come and help with the food,' said Susanne, following Julia to the kitchen.

Anton and Alice went to the terrace to play cards before dinner. Erik looked at his father-in-law. 'Would you like a beer?' he asked.

'Why not,' said Göran.

Erik came back with cold beers for Göran and Anders. The mood at the summer house had improved after Anders arrived. Julia seemed to have relaxed a bit, as if it helped to throw other people into the mix.

Göran took a big swig of beer and looked at the tarn.

'We always used to call it the Pond when Julia was little. It's probably too big to be called a marsh, and it's not really swamp-like. I haven't been out here in a long time.'

'Why not?' asked Erik. 'It's such a great place.'

Göran looked suddenly anxious.

'We've just never taken the time,' he said at last.

'Did you go swimming there? In the tarn?' asked Erik.

'Maybe when it was newly dredged. I wouldn't recommend it. So, how's work going?'

'I'm not too sure. These are tough times.'

'Yes, I read about that in the paper. But everything's okay with you, right?'

'Absolutely. I'm not in any danger.'

'Good. It was a smart decision to study IT. There will always be jobs in that field. By the way, I read something about your former colleague in the paper. Did you hear that he sold part of his company to Japanese investors?'

'I heard something like that.'

'A billion euros. He's going to make a billion on the deal. Well, not him personally, but the company. And a lot of it will go to taxes, of course. Still. What a deal.'

'That's a lot of money,' Erik agreed.

'You could have been part of that,' said Göran.

'It's not that simple,' said Erik.

'No, I suppose not,' said Göran.

Julia was in the kitchen with her mother, making dinner. Susanne was a good cook, and she had a vegetable garden at home. She also had a pedagogical streak, which meant that she enjoyed giving instructions, although Julia noticed that today she was being a little careless and having to improvise.

Susanne was already immersed in her daily monologue. This time she was talking about her latest project which she had reluctantly accepted – or so she claimed – because she could tell that no one else would be able to do the job as well as she could. Julia had long ago stopped taking any interest in her mother's work. She would merely nod occasionally while trying to think about something else, pretending she was listening to the radio with some overly talkative middle-aged woman on the air.

'So initially I thought about turning it down, but then they asked me to stay on for another year, with a higher salary and a bigger office, so now I've decided to take the offer, and we have a lot of fun projects planned for the autumn. But good Lord, I can't bear the thought of going to China again. It makes me tired just thinking about it.'

Julia didn't say a word as she focused on the cooking.

'This is the dish I usually offer my guests from China,' said Susanne as she picked up slices of air-dried ham and arranged them around an avocado salad.

Her fingers were shiny with olive oil. Susanne's Chinese guests were a perennial joke in the family. She had friends in Shanghai whom she'd met through her job. When Julia was a child, she'd always celebrated Christmas with her parents and her brother and a handful of excessively polite Chinese university teachers.

'He seems rather lackadaisical,' said Susanne.

'Who do you mean?'

'Erik's brother. We've never actually been properly introduced.'

Julia had always been bothered by the way her mother would inspect someone from top to toe, as if she were doing a scan of their socio-economic position and lifestyle. At first Julia had thought it was merely a superficial habit, but later she began to wonder whether it was actually a sophisticated computation which Susanne silently carried out. If Susanne were set down in the bush somewhere in the Kalahari, thought Julia, she would no doubt quickly learn the methods needed to recognise hostile tribes.

'So, are we ready?' Susanne asked.

'I think so. I'm just going to let the meat rest for a bit,' replied Julia.

'Oh no, look, I spilled something.'

Susanne tried to wipe off a spot of salad dressing from her dress, but she only spread the oil even more.

'Wait a minute and I'll get a damp paper towel,' said Julia. 'Is that a new dress?'

'Yes, I bought it in Paris. It's always so hard to find anything in my size. But there's a boutique in the gay quarter – what's it called? – and I always go there. At any rate, I saw this dress in the window, and of course it cost a fortune, but it's such good quality. You can throw it in the washing machine at forty degrees and it comes out like new. With my job, I need dresses like this.'

Julia rubbed a paper towel on the spot. Susanne took the paper from her and rubbed some more.

'I saw so many beautiful dresses there. Do you think Alice would like to have something from Paris, by the way? It's a shame she always wears black. But maybe that's the current fashion. Do her friends look the same way? With black hair hanging in their eyes?'

'Not really. It's something Alice came up with. She's a very independent sort of girl.'

'But she's so quiet. I'd like to see her smile once in a while,' said Susanne.

'She smiles when she feels like it,' said Julia.

'Sure. Maybe. Well, Anton is just the same, at least. Though he's put on weight.'

Julia noticed herself tuning out. She couldn't stand to hear any more.

'I don't think I'm going to be able to get this out,' said Susanne now, tossing the paper in the rubbish bin under the sink. 'By the way, how are things with you and Erik?'

The question came out of nowhere, and Julia was annoyed. No matter how much she disliked her mother's interference, Susanne often seemed to have a sixth sense for what was worrying her.

'I'm not really sure. I suppose things are okay. I don't know. Maybe we're going through some sort of crisis.'

She actually didn't want to talk to her mother about it. Susanne would always make use of whatever she said. Her words would turn up in some later conversation, when she was least expecting it, to be used against her.

'Oh well, it's probably not serious. People go through crises and come out the other side. God only knows that your father and I have certainly had our share of problems.'

Julia knew what she meant because her mother always told her about all her marital crises. Also the times when, according to Susanne, her parents had been on the verge of divorce.

'Yes, but this isn't the same thing,' said Julia. 'I'm wondering whether we belong together at all. Maybe we've grown apart.'

'The two of you are very different,' said Susanne. 'He may be a little placid.'

'Erik?'

'But just think how good he is with the children.'

Julia didn't respond. She picked up the casserole dish of potatoes and headed for the door.

They were all seated at the table out in the yard, helping themselves to Susanne's avocado salad and the steaks that Erik had grilled. There was also herring and potatoes, along with chilled schnapps and white wine.

Alice was checking Instagram on her mobile phone. She hadn't given a lot of thought to her birthday, but it definitely felt better to be thirteen than twelve. When Leo had asked her how old she was, she'd said thirteen, so she was hoping he wouldn't find out that her birthday wasn't until today.

'What are you looking at?' asked Julia. 'Can't you put your phone away while we're eating? Especially when it's your birthday, and everything.'

'I'm not looking at anything,' said Alice.

'Then put the phone away.'

'Kids these days. They can't be without their phones,' said Julia's father. Then he started in on a lengthy harangue about why he preferred phones with real buttons. Susanne poured herself more wine. She had sat down next to Anders and was questioning him about his trip to Vietnam.

'One day I rode a motorcycle up into the mountains. There's a tradition that it's good luck to drink booze with Westerners. So in every village I came to, I had to stop for a drink. Even the police officers offered me schnapps,' he said.

Susanne, who quickly lost interest in other people's stories, started recounting her own anecdote, about the time she was in a village outside Shanghai and ate grilled songbirds. Julia had heard that story at least fifty times.

'But first they brought a little bowl of blood that they wanted the honoured guests to drink.'

Anton listened with fascination.

'What kind of blood, Granny?'

'I don't know. Maybe from a snake.'

'Yuck,' said Anton.

Julia was annoyed and tired and suggested they should sing happy birthday to Alice.

'Could you put away your phone now that we're going to have cake?' she said to her daughter.

Alice shook her head.

'She's chatting with Leo,' Anton whispered to his grandmother.

'Who's Leo?' asked Susanne.

'Mamma, do you remember the Segerkvists?' asked Julia. 'The girl named Marika that I used to play with? Leo is her son.'

Susanne suddenly had a blank look on her face, as if realising she'd forgotten to switch off the coffee maker back home. She asked to see Alice's mobile, but Alice quickly stuck it in her pocket.

'You wrote about her in your book,' said Göran.

'She lives down by the water. In that collective.'

'We haven't seen them for decades,' said Susanne. 'I think they moved to Åbo, or someplace like that. Are they here for the whole summer? Her parents too?' asked Susanne.

'No, just Marika and her husband. Her mother died of cancer. And her father is remarried,' replied Julia.

'Aha,' said Susanne.

'What?' asked Julia.

'Nothing. So where's that cake?'

By nine o'clock the sauna was heated up, and Anders couldn't be found. He had excused himself after dinner and hadn't returned.

'I think we'll go ahead without him,' Erik told Göran. 'My brother isn't so good in social situations.'

They stayed in the sauna a long time, almost an hour. Then they walked down to the rocks together and jumped in the water.

It was cold, but the sea had a sobering effect. During the day a thin mist had formed in the sky. Erik had had a few beers and was feeling a little tipsy. The dark sea undulated, silhouetted against the milky white clouds. The salty water tasted good as it slid between his lips.

The silence came as a surprise to Erik. It had never been this quiet here before. No seagulls, only the gentle lapping of the water, which made the world seem smaller, closer.

Göran got out of the water and picked up a towel.

'I'm going back. Are you coming with me?'

'In a bit,' said Erik.

He sat on his towel and stared out across the bay. After a while he heard a door open at the house on the other side. Kati came out of her sauna with a towel wrapped around her. Steam rose off her body, and she was glistening with moisture in the bright evening.

When she went down to the water for a swim, she turned and caught sight of him. He couldn't make himself look away until she threw herself into the water and began swimming.

He stood up and watched for a while. Just as he was about to leave, he heard the door of the sauna across the bay open again. The sound echoed. And then Anders came out, naked, carrying a beer in his hand. At first Erik didn't recognise him without any clothes on. He'd gained weight since the spring, yet there could be no doubt. The beard, the slightly stooped posture, the skinny legs. Erik was so surprised that he couldn't think of a thing to say. He couldn't even shout a greeting. He merely backed away and headed for the woods.

10

ANDERS HAD SPENT HIS first three days at Mjölkviken down at the beach by himself. He came back to the house in the evening, often sitting at the small table near the tarn, talking to Julia or watching the kids play cards on the rocks. Erik had wandered around, trying to engage the other family members in various activities, but all of them seemed to prefer being on their own. Anders thought Erik seemed distant and uneasy about something, so he was overcompensating by getting up each morning and announcing exactly what he thought of the weather and things in general.

The first night Anders had sat outdoors until late, with a blanket wrapped around his shoulders, pondering what he should do with his life. At two in the morning, Alice had suddenly come out to the terrace, walking around as she looked at her mobile. Anders sat motionless at the table, in the shadows, hoping she wouldn't notice him because he didn't want to startle her. Apparently Alice was also having trouble sleeping.

After a while she went back inside. Anders stayed where he was, looking at his own phone. He followed Alice on Instagram, and saw that she'd posted a photo. Anders recognised it: a picture of The Cure and the video for 'Friday I'm in Love'. Underneath she'd written: '#robertsmith #cutiepie #happy'. He was happy for her, thinking it was nice that at least somebody in this family seemed happy.

By four thirty the sky was brightening. Heat rose from the moss near the tarn, spreading across the dark surface of the water until it finally reached the table where he was sitting. He decided to go down to the beach to watch the sun come up.

He walked along the path towards the bay. The sun coloured the sky pink, and the rocks glowed a lovely red. This type of landscape always made him think about religious people and their belief that God could be found in nature. A perfect Nordic dawn. But it was incomparably beautiful, that couldn't be denied. And the morning was so quiet and still, as if summer were holding its breath while everyone slept. He walked along the shore, peering at the water, and then glancing up at the grey house.

He hadn't expected to see anyone sitting on the terrace this early in the morning. He had to look twice before it really sunk in that a woman was sitting in an armchair next to the door of the house.

She had undoubtedly seen him, she must have done, but she gave no sign that she had. She merely sat there, wrapped in a blanket, as if she were focusing on some invisible film being shown on the horizon.

Anders went over to the house, but not even then did she react.

'Beautiful morning,' he said, thinking that at any moment he'd discover the woman was only a doll that someone had set on the armchair.

She turned her head and said something, but he couldn't make out what it was because she spoke so quietly.

He went closer.

'What did you say?' he asked.

'I said it almost looks like a picture from a poster or some kind of religious journal,' she told him.

'Exactly what I was thinking,' he replied.

He went up the steps to shake hands with her. She remained sitting in the chair, wrapped in the blanket, and made no move to get up. She held out her hand.

'Kati,' she said.

'Anders,' he said. 'I suppose you might be tired of seeing the sun rise, if you see it every morning.'

'I don't think I could ever grow tired of the dawn. It's probably some sort of primal instinct that makes it seem so hypnotic.'

She was beautiful, with dark hair and sharp features. Right now she didn't seem to be aware of things around her. She didn't look at him, didn't stare.

For the first time in a long while, Anders was feeling good. He took a chance and began talking to her. 'I hope I'm not disturbing you,' he said.

She hesitated for a moment, then smiled. 'Not at all. I was just thinking of getting up to make some coffee. Would you like a cup?'

It was a big house, much too big for one person, but there was no sign that anyone else was living there. It looked as if someone had started furnishing the place but never finished. Paintings leaned against the walls, books were piled up, there was a large sofa but no coffee table. Clothes were strewn across the floor and books were stacked on a chair next to the sofa. A tennis racket lay near the door. He saw a TV and a stairway leading up to the attic. There was also a spacious kitchen with a lovely big table covered with piles of newspapers, a milk carton and lots of crumbs.

She went into the kitchen and put on the coffee. Anders stood in the doorway for a moment, wondering if he dared go in.

'You can sit over there,' she said.

He took that to be a command, so he sat down at the kitchen table. He glanced at the stacks of books. Mostly Nordic detective novels.

'Have you read all these?' he asked.

'I've started some of them,' she said.

For a long time neither of them spoke. He looked out of the window at the bay and the morning.

'You're staying up in the house in the woods, aren't you?' she said.

'Yes. Or rather, my brother and his family are staying there. I've just dropped by to visit.'

'I've seen them occasionally, when they're down on the rocks. They're like a family out of a catalogue. She's so beautiful – the mother, I mean.'

'Julia,' said Anders.

'Here,' she said, handing him a cup of coffee.

They went out to the terrace to have their coffee. The morning sun and clouds made the landscape change shape every ten minutes. Shadows changed places, the colours on the rocks shifted, the sea turned from grey to blue without warning. It was no more than six o'clock.

'Do you also have trouble sleeping at night? I mean, since it's obvious you've been sitting out here for a while,' said Anders.

'I sleep only two or three hours a night. I usually get up if I can't sleep. Now that it's finally warmer, it's easier to sit outside,' she said.

Her tone of voice indicated that she didn't want to say more about the matter, yet he couldn't help himself.

'What do you do?' he asked.

'What do I do?'

'I mean, what sort of work do you do?'

'Nothing,' she said.

He paused for a moment.

'Me neither, actually. I mean, I'm not on holiday, or anything like that. I really do nothing.'

'What will you do when you're finished doing nothing?'

'I don't know. What about you?' he asked.

She laughed. 'I don't know.'

She didn't laugh long, but it was enough to make warmth spread through Anders' body.

He continued: 'I'm starting to feel that it's not so great doing nothing. For a long time I thought it would be okay, but I don't think it's really good for me. It may be that work has its plus side, after all.'

'I've seen your brother's family. I thought it looked pretty good. Doing something, I mean.'

'Even though you said they look as if they're out of a catalogue.'

'Yes, they do.'

'But aren't those types of families a little unpleasant?'

'I didn't think about that,' she said.

'My brother is afraid of everyone who isn't happy and positive. That's why he starts each day by adjusting the mood in the room. He tries to make everybody feel the same way he does. But deep inside he's not happy, and for that reason he doesn't notice the impact it has on all the others.'

'So what about you? Are you happy?' she asked.

Anders stared out across the water.

It was like a bubble. A warm and inexplicable bubble they entered that morning and remained in for a while. Kati got up to fetch more coffee and a blanket for Anders, and then they sat on the terrace for a long time, chatting only sporadically. He didn't ask her anything specific. They talked a little about feelings they had, though without anchoring them in any real examples. Their discussion took on an almost abstract form, so that when Anders talked about how much he liked black coffee, it almost sounded like a metaphor. Everything became a symbol, an innuendo.

Gradually he began telling her about himself, making Kati laugh many times. He explained how he'd bought copies of Nina Björk's 1996 feminist classic *Under the Pink Duvet* for every member of his family. His paternal grandfather actually read the book and declared Swedes to be idiots because they believed gender was socially, and not biologically, defined. ('Seems like this whole country is nothing but fags these days.')

They talked about Anders' brother and his brother's family.

'Erik is someone who never loses control. Never. I don't understand how Julia puts up with him. Did you know she's an author?'

'Maybe they complement each other.'

'Maybe. But I can see it in their eyes – they're each in their own world,' said Anders.

'I have a hard time believing there's anyone who isn't. That's part of life. In some way we're always immersed in ourselves. A person with no boundaries would merely be living through his partner, which wouldn't be good either. Human beings aren't meant to merge completely. That wouldn't work.'

'Maybe not. I don't know. I don't really know them all that well. Or how they are together. I just feel like giving my brother a good shake once in a while. It's as if he has never suffered a significant blow to the head.'

'Why do you talk so much about them?'

'What? I do?'

'Yes. Instead of talking about yourself, you keep talking about what your brother is like. Speaking of boundaries … I doubt very much he lives through you.'

'Maybe you're right,' he said.

'You asked me earlier what I do. I'm a therapist. I used to be, that is,' she said.

'Ah. That explains a lot,' he replied, laughing.

When it was lunchtime, she asked if he'd like to stay and have something to eat.

'I think they're waiting for me over there, but I could come back later,' he said.

'Okay,' she said. And he stood up and left.

Back at the summer house Julia and Erik asked Anders what he'd been doing. He told them he'd gone out for a long walk.

'You must have left really early because you were gone by the time I woke up,' said Julia.

'Yeah. I couldn't sleep. I've been up since five.'

He slipped out and went back to the beach after lunch, but he didn't tell anyone where he was going.

Kati was sitting in the same place, in her armchair on the terrace.

'I've got to go to the supermarket later today, but it's not that important. I could wait until tomorrow,' she told him.

'I could drive you there, if you like. We could borrow my brother's car.'

'That would be great.'

He thought – and he'd been thinking this since morning – that he'd like to go to bed with her, but when he imagined himself doing that, taking the first step, it seemed impossible.

He'd felt so relaxed and calm all morning, in a way he hadn't experienced in ages, but now he felt nervous and awkward. Overweight Anders, ugly Anders, hopeless and impossible Anders who ate nothing but crisps and always felt sorry for himself.

He made a real effort to find his way back to the bubble they'd shared earlier by saying something that felt genuine and real, something from his very core. It was that sort of day. He wanted to find a truth. He sat down in the armchair next to her and pulled half of her blanket over himself.

'Tell me a little about yourself,' she said.

'How much time do you have?' he asked.

'I've got all day.'

'Well, you're asking me a difficult question. Who am I? People always say that I'm a diamond in the rough, that I have talent but I don't know what to do with it. Sometimes when I meet women, I think that's what they see: someone they can rein in a bit so I'll reach my full potential. But what if it's simply because I'm already polished as much as I'll ever be? What if I'm never going to be any better than I already am?'

Neither of them shifted position as they reclined in their chairs. Anders gazed out at the sea, feeling as though he were able to speak with complete freedom. There were no demands to say the right thing or to say something merely because that's what a certain person wanted to hear. He listened to the rushing of the sea, letting his words spill out into the clear air. He felt totally in the moment.

'I feel so calm here.'

'Sometimes you have to look at something outside of yourself. I've noticed that's a really effective method. So you need to think of something or someone who makes you happy, maybe a specific place where you like to go, instead of trying to find the "real you". Then it's easy to lose yourself.'

Anders focused, trying to summon pictures in his mind of places where he was happy, trying to pinpoint what made him feel safe.

'As I said, I think it's great to be here right now.'

'That's a start,' said Kati.

'And I don't know what it is, but sometimes I think I'd like to be enclosed. Do you know what I mean? Enclosed in a dark embrace, wrapped in softness.'

'I understand.'

'I'm not sure you really do. Oh, this sounds so ridiculous ...'

'No, not at all.'

'Am I making any kind of sense?' he asked.

'Yes, you are. For a whole lot of us, it's basically all about wanting to be enclosed and loved, about feeling safe and warm.'

Anders thought about the times when he'd tried, when he'd truly opened up to the possibility, but it had never worked out because he never chose the right person. Like the woman he'd talked to in the pub in Hanoi. He'd ended up sitting next to her by chance, and she had looked so beautiful in the dim light of the pub, and she had smiled at him – and that had been that. She had given him something that night, she was someone with whom he could share a moment, but afterwards it had become difficult and complicated. Until at last he was the one who was forced to console and explain, because she'd dreamed of sharing a life with him in Finland, though he'd had no interest in doing anything like that. Or what about Karin, the teacher at the community college where he'd attended classes one winter? He'd had a difficult relationship with her because the whole time he'd wanted much more than she had, until he'd finally realised that she was only paying attention to him because it was a way for her to endure her life, and she did the same thing with several others.

These kinds of experiences had given him the feeling that it was best to shut down and not take any risks, since all risks hurled him out into a stormy sea where he eventually lost himself.

'I don't think feeling safe is for everyone,' he said now. 'Maybe some people are made so they can never feel safe.'

'I don't think so. Did you feel that way as a child?'

'I was sick for large parts of my childhood. I had stomach problems. So I quickly learned to pretend, to say that every-thing was fine because I couldn't deal with all the questions and worry. And it was embarrassing to be sick all the time, especially because my illness meant I had to keep running to the toilet. I constantly felt ashamed, and I had to keep the shame to myself, because I didn't want to upset anyone else.'

'Would you like more coffee?' she asked.

'Sure. That would great. Thanks,' he said.

When Julia's parents came to visit a couple of days later, Anders couldn't focus on the birthday celebration for Alice, no matter how hard he tried. All he could think about was seeing Kati again. Finally, after they'd all had a piece of birthday cake, he excused himself, saying that he was going for a walk.

11

LEO CAME OVER TO SEE Alice on the morning after the party. She'd gone down to the road several times to look for him, but she hadn't dared go as far as his family's property, afraid of making a fool of herself. They'd started following each other on Instagram, but otherwise had communicated only by liking each other's pictures.

'Why don't you invite him over?' her mother had asked, as if Alice had any say in the matter. She felt annoyed that her mother even knew about this, and talked about it as if it were any of her business.

The whole thing was beyond Alice's control, yet she liked the feeling it gave her. Not only the warmth in her body when she thought about looking at the nape of his neck as they'd walked down to the beach on that first evening, but also that she had something here in Mjölkviken that no one in her school had. That feeling. She'd be able to go home after the summer holidays and talk about him – or she might not; it really didn't matter one way or the other. More important was the fact that this was hers. Like the ring that she'd found, it was enough just to know about it. That's why she didn't want her mother to talk about Leo as if he was just anybody.

She listened to 'Titanium' and felt the blood rushing through her body as she walked down to the road, but she turned around before she got there and went back to the summer house. She stretched out on her bed to read a book, although she couldn't really concentrate.

Leo's mother had come over to visit one evening. She and Julia had coffee out on the terrace and then switched to gin and tonic. They talked about old memories, and it was so annoying to listen to them.

Alice's mother had laughed way too loud at something stupid and then said to her: 'Why don't you go over to see Leo?'

'He's home with his father and probably totally bored,' said Marika. 'I'm sure he'd welcome your company.'

'You could take Anton with you,' said her mother.

Then Julia and Marika had started talking about how anti-social kids were these days. They recalled running around the whole area, from one house to another, and playing with boys when they were kids. At that point Alice didn't feel like hearing any more, so she put her headphones in.

No, she thought, he should come here instead. And this time she wouldn't let Anton tag along. She pictured herself with Leo, taking a path that led deeper into the woods, or on an outing to the public beach, just the two of them, alone. And he would understand when she talked about school and her friends; he would say 'that's exactly how it is,' and they'd laugh at all the idiots in the world.

But he didn't make an appearance that day, or the next day either.

Then on Tuesday he turned up, looking happy and a little shy yet delightfully nonchalant. He stood over her as she lay on the mattress in her ridiculous swimsuit, which made it impossible for her to turn around. Instead, she had to peer up at him from an angle, turning her head 180 degrees, since she didn't want to lie on her back to look up at him. He blocked out the sun as he asked Alice whether she'd like to go down to the beach. She nodded.

Then she got up and put on the big black T-shirt with 'The

Cure' on the front which she'd left on the rocks next to the mattress. She picked up her canvas bag that held her books and other things, since it seemed like this was going to be a real outing. Then they headed off together without saying a word.

Anders and the woman were together down there. They were sitting on the woman's terrace, talking. The others didn't know he was there, but Alice had seen him on that first evening. Now he waved to her. She pretended not to see him.

Instead, she fixed her eyes on Leo's downy nape, though she quickly averted her eyes when he noticed she was looking at him. He had freckles and was squinting at the sun. Alice sniffed at her hand. It smelled of suntan lotion. She was glad she had rubbed some on her skin.

'I would have come over before,' Leo said, 'but Pappa wanted me to stay inside and do my homework. And that made me so cross.'

'Aren't you on holiday?' asked Alice.

'Yes, but Pappa has decided to homeschool me. Mamma and Pappa think it's hard on me because I keep having to change schools. So they decided it would be easier if Pappa teaches me. We might be moving again.'

'Where?' she asked, feeling her stomach lurch with fear. But she should have expected this. She knew already that the summer would come to an end, and then it wouldn't matter where he lived.

'I'm not sure, but if I know my father, it'll be some place that's as remote as possible, probably somewhere in Scotland. Or here. He wants to be self-supporting.'

'Here?'

'Pappa wants to move here. He says it gives him a sense of calm that he can't find anywhere else.'

'But you don't even have running water,' said Alice, although she was happy to hear of this possibility.

'That's probably what Pappa likes. He says we can wash in the sauna every day. He's been talking to somebody about raising dogs and keeping chickens, and he wants to start here.'

'How do you feel about that?' asked Alice.

She'd never had to think about suddenly moving away or living without running water. It made her like Leo even more; it made her think that he needed somebody, somebody he could talk to. And she wanted to be that person.

They stopped now. They were near the rocks on the south side of the bay. When he sat down, his feet dangled in the air, unable to reach the ground. He had on a pair of old Adidas, more worn out than any trainers the boys in her class had, and she thought that was the difference between Leo and her class-mates: he didn't care. He might have shoes that were tattered, he might have a smudge of dirt on his chin, but he was stronger than anyone she knew. Now he tucked his hair behind his ears. His hair was like gold, not white and shiny but like burnished gold, as if made up of several colours even though there was only one.

'I'm so fucking tired of my parents, the way they can never make up their minds. It's like every day they think up something new in life, and it's always the most important thing in the world. I've never had a friend for more than a year and a half,' he said, but it didn't sound as if he felt sorry for himself. He actually sounded angry, the way a grown-up might sound angry about something.

'When I was little I always dreamed of living in the country. If you guys move here, we could at least see each other in the summertime,' said Alice.

'That's true,' he said, smiling at her. Then he turned sad. She could see it in his eyes, and she had a great urge to jump up and give him a hug.

'Do you like music?' she asked.

'That depends,' he said.
'Want to listen to some?'

They sat down in a cleft in the rocks where they would be warm and sheltered from the wind. Alice had a hard time deciding what to play first. She went through all her playlists, but she thought the song choices were too revealing – she didn't want him to think she was trying to tell him something.

Finally she chose an album that her mother liked too. Nina Simone. She sometimes listened to it when she wanted to feel totally calm.

'I don't really listen to this very often, but I think it's great,' she said, pulling her headphones out of her pocket and starting the music. *Black is the colour of my true love's hair.* They lay down on the rocks so their heads were almost touching. *I love the ground on which he stands.* She thought about Leo's hair and wanted to take a picture of the two of them, but he might not like it. She thought he might not like taking selfies.

Anton had been inside the old playhouse on the property, looking out of the window when Leo walked past. He was glad Leo hadn't seen him. He didn't want anyone to think of him as a boy who played on his own inside a kids' playhouse. In reality, Anton had taken his old Nintendo DS with him and was playing a Pokémon game that had been a birthday present when he turned seven. He'd hardly played with it back then, but now he'd rediscovered the game and had been playing for several days. He had only a few levels left. He liked the little playhouse because it was dark inside. The sun was too bright for him to play the game outdoors.

When Leo and Alice headed for the beach, Anton left the game in the playhouse and followed them. At first he pretended he was tracking an animal, trying to spot their footprints in the sand. He followed them down to the shore and watched Alice and Leo walk across the rocks and then sit down somewhere out of sight. He wondered how he could spy on them without being seen. He realised he'd have to go into the woods next to the bay and get closer from the other direction, as if he were manoeuvring himself in a computer game.

It was warm and dry, not at all like it'd been the past few weeks. Now the sun was blazing, which made him thirsty and long for a cool breeze from the sea. He walked past an old rotting rowing-boat abandoned in the woods, then headed for the rocks on the south side. He hid behind several pine trees, trying to spot Leo and Alice.

Here in the woods he could hear his own breathing and pulse, small twigs dropping to the ground, the steady rushing from the sea and the gulls hovering over the shoreline. When he'd almost reached the edge of the woods, where the rocks started, he saw them.

They were lying on the rocks with their eyes closed. Not speaking, focused on the music coming from the headphones. They didn't move, and he thought at first that they might be dead. He stood there for a long time, breathing as quietly as he could, straining to be as motionless as a statue. But finally he got tired of looking at them, so he sat down.

Anton sometimes wondered whether his brain might function differently from everyone else's. He wasn't like his classmate Elliot who could concentrate on whatever the teachers said and always got top marks in everything. Anton didn't have trouble in school. He got good grades, but he was always more interested in what was happening inside him.

For a while he worried that he might be taking part in a film. He wondered whether it might be possible that the world around him didn't really exist. Or rather: that everything he did was being filmed and someone was watching the film of his life.

And maybe even listening to his thoughts. If that was true, he wondered whether that meant the eavesdropping would stop if he discovered it. If somebody was listening to his thoughts, that would mean they were also listening when he thought about them listening.

He had brooded about this when he decided he liked a girl in his class. It felt as if everybody knew. That was a year ago now, in the springtime.

Her name was Agnes. She had long brown hair and sat two seats in front of him.

The only person he told was Iiris. And that was only because she'd asked him whether he liked anyone, as if she already knew the answer.

A few days later his phone rang.

He was home alone, sitting on the sofa, and he'd just heated up some pierogies in the microwave. He picked up the phone. It was afternoon, and the sun shone through the big windows in the living room. The school day had just ended.

'Hi, this is Maija.'

Maija was also in Anton's class.

'I'm here with Agnes. She wants to be your girlfriend.'

What she said seemed true and yet not true. Maija giggled, and someone else in the background did too. But what if it really was true? Anton froze and could hardly say a word.

'She does?' he said cautiously.

Suddenly he was no longer sure that's what he wanted. It seemed too overwhelming now that it was happening in reality.

'She wants to know if you could meet her at four o'clock at the school,' said Maija. Anton said he could.

It was only three, so he nervously roamed through the flat for almost an hour. He went to his father's cabinet and took out a bottle of cologne and sprayed a little on his neck.

His stomach was churning as he walked to school to meet

Agnes. He had combed his hair and put on his favourite jacket. It seemed to take much longer than normal, and for some reason he kept feeling like he should stop and look at everything. He walked past the shoemaker's shop and the antiques shop. He looked both ways several times before crossing the street, then walked past the big car park and entered the schoolyard.

Agnes was nowhere in sight. Instead, he saw a girl from a different class – he didn't know her name – with Maija and Iiris.

'Hi, Anton. Are you here to meet Agnes?'

He nodded, sensing at once that this was a mistake. Nausea surged in his throat.

'Did you really believe that?' asked Maija. Iiris stood next to her, looking very pale. She didn't say a word.

'Did you really think Agnes wanted to be your girlfriend? We're the ones who called you,' said Maija. She and the other girl started laughing.

'It was just a joke!' they yelled after Anton as he left. 'Can't you take a joke?'

All the way home he had to hold back his tears. Then he threw himself on his parents' bed and cried for a long time, hitting himself on the head for being so stupid. He hated Iiris and her friends. The only consolation was that maybe they hadn't talked to Agnes. Maybe she knew nothing about all this.

It seemed unfair that Alice had a friend. If she hadn't been here, maybe Leo would have played Nintendo with him instead. But Alice was the one who had Leo. He was hers now, and she didn't want to share him with anyone.

Finally Anton heard them get up and brush themselves off. They jumped back up on the rocks and headed for the tennis courts. He waited a few minutes and then followed.

He thought about how it would be to live in South Korea,

because lately he'd seen so many YouTube videos with South Korean guys talking about games, and he thought it seemed so cool there. Would it be possible to live in South Korea and earn a living by making YouTube videos? Or did you have to be Asian to do that?

As he walked through the woods towards the tennis courts, he thought about all these things. At the same time he imagined how he'd post a video on YouTube in which he talked about the game he'd been playing all week, and he constructed long sentences in English in which he explained how to make your way through the different levels, and the woods all around became more like a level in a video game, and that instantly made the game even more fun, as he imagined how he had to make his way past various obstacles to reach the tennis courts.

He reached them just as Leo and Alice disappeared into a root cellar. He watched as Leo held the door open for Alice, who ducked her head and stepped inside.

Alice saw there was a bare light bulb hanging from the ceiling. Presumably a wire was buried in the earth and connected to the electricity at the house. Leo turned on the light and they stood in the glow, looking each other in the eyes. Then he turned it off, and Alice instantly thought that felt better. She didn't even flinch when he took her hand in the dark.

'All right?' he asked, raising his other hand to lightly touch her breast. 'Just tell me if you want me to stop.'

He lifted up her T-shirt and ran his hand over her bra. She liked that. It made her feel warm. He moved his hand inside her bra, and she felt his cold, soft hand on her skin. The darkness was like velvet, as if she could sink into it, like water.

Afterwards she couldn't remember whether she was the one who took the initiative, or whether he did, but he showed her what to do with her hand. It didn't last long, and there was a stain on her T-shirt afterwards. She washed it off in the sea, and then they went swimming together, heading away from shore until the waves got big and the water was so deep and cold that they were forced to turn around.

part three

nature

1

EACH MORNING ANDERS would quietly walk across the sand to Kati's house. She was often sitting on the terrace, and would get up to fetch him a cup of coffee when he appeared. Then they would usually sit outside for a long time without saying anything, merely looking at the sea and the morning light, which looked different every day.

July brought perfect summer weather. In the city it was too hot, but out here at the sea there was always a cool breeze that offered respite, even on the hottest afternoons. The water quickly warmed up, and even Anton ventured in for a swim, often with Leo and Alice, who took long walks around the area or sat on the rocks and listened to music.

One morning Anders was sitting with Kati as he read on his mobile about the collective at the beach. On Google he'd found an old article in the *Guardian* describing Chris Blackwood's movement in detail, with photos of the Scottish Highlands, in which Leo and Marika could also be seen. The family was described as 'neo-hippies'. They were said to have updated the flower-power message, though for them it wasn't about 'peace & love', but about a sense of humility towards the earth's limitations.

In the interview Chris quoted from the old Peter Gabriel tune 'Here Comes the Flood'.

In the photo, a somewhat younger Chris stood on a hill, wearing a Norwegian woollen sweater.

'Imagine that we humans are on board a huge spaceship,' he told the interviewer. 'Meaning we're the crew of the spaceship, and we're completely dependent on the life-support systems of the ship, including access to food and water. But we've managed to sabotage these systems, and none of us knows how long we can survive before the food runs out. Yet even without us, the ship will continue to travel through space.'

His background was also described. He grew up as the only child of academic parents. His father was an amateur bird-watcher, and nature had been a constant part of Chris's upbringing.

After secondary school he'd gone to Oxford and studied philosophy, politics and economics during some of the same years as David Cameron. During his time at university, he was known as a liberal debater among student circles, representing the leading trends of the time. Afterwards, he spent several successful years in finance, only to do an about-face in the nineties when he joined the anti-globalisation movement. In 1999, for instance, he worked as a volunteer during the WTO demonstrations in Seattle. The *Guardian* article also mentioned that he'd met his Finnish life partner, Marika, at a conference in Norway.

The article was five years old, and when Anders did another Google search, he saw that information from more recent years presented a less coherent picture. He found newer articles that dealt with the overpopulation of the planet and the problem this presented, articles in which Chris quoted the controversial Finnish ecologist Pentti Linkola and seemed to advocate for a society governed by a small elite. It was hard to get a true sense of Chris Blackwood and his movement, which was most often mentioned only in obscure blogs. His own blog hadn't been updated very often over the past few years. It consisted of disparate thoughts about what 'de-civilisation' meant, as well as minor efforts to write poems in line with that principle. He seemed to have developed his own vocabulary, which was supposed to form some sort of primal language.

Anders read aloud selected passages to Kati.

'You'd think they would write their messages in the sand instead of on the internet,' he said.

'I think that's what they actually do,' said Kati. 'They spend a lot of time down there on the sand, although the words get erased almost instantly.'

They laughed.

Just as they'd finished their second cup of coffee of the morning, they heard muted trumpet blasts coming from the neighbours.

'Is that a didgeridoo?' asked Anders.

'I think it's something similar,' said Kati.

'Maybe that's their way of announcing that it's time for lunch. Or maybe they don't believe in lunch, maybe that's too modern for them. It sounds more like some sort of sexual thing. "Time for today's orgy." Why do you think all "back-to-nature" movements are so obsessed with sex?'

'You're asking the wrong person,' said Kati.

'All extreme movements make the mistake of thinking they can change the world overnight. They don't realise that the majority of people don't get it. That's why it never amounts to anything, because the group doesn't have enough followers.'

For a while neither of them spoke.

'Did you get any sleep last night?' he asked then. He knew Kati had a hard time sleeping, and that she sat out here on the terrace to rest.

'I actually slept a little longer than usual. I didn't wake up until six, and strangely enough I was hungry. I'm not usually hungry in the morning. Or at least, that hasn't happened in a long time,' she said.

He realised he wanted to know more about her. He wanted to know everything she was willing to tell him. She sat and stared at the sea, occasionally taking a sip of coffee.

'I don't know very much about you.'

'What do you want to know?'

'For instance, what are you doing here? We meet every day and sit here and read books and talk, but I don't know what you really do. It doesn't seem like you're on holiday.'

'No, I'm not,' she said. 'I'm on sick leave.'

'Do you want to talk about it?'

'There's not really much to tell you. I fell into a depression and came here in May.'

'Do you have a family?' he asked.

'Two children, but the younger one also moved away from home last year, so now I'm alone.'

Kati told Anders a little about her life, about her children, about her job as a therapist. Anders was aware he shouldn't ask whether she had a husband. Maybe she didn't, and there would be nothing strange about that. He felt a certain shamefaced joy about meeting her here like this – both of them alone and in need of someone to talk to. Or was he merely imagining that? He didn't really understand why she was so welcoming towards him, or what about him interested her.

'Have you talked to them?' Anders asked.

'Who do you mean?'

'The people down there at the beach.'

'The only thing I know is that they run around on the sand every evening. But they're probably harmless. I think they just drink too much and take drugs. That's the way people end up. But I feel sorry for the boy. Sometimes I wonder whether I should call social services. I haven't yet. I get the impression they'd think I'm nuts.'

'Why's that?'

'Well, because all I do is sit out here day after day, doing nothing.'

'They think you're the odd one, while we sit here and laugh at their didgeridoo-penis extension.'

Kati laughed.

When it was lunchtime, Anders stayed at Kati's house. She thawed out the last of what was in her freezer – some French fries and fish sticks – and they ate the food out on the terrace.

'That's all I've got left. And these fish sticks are probably two years old.'

'Maybe we could borrow a car and drive to the supermarket later today. Would you like that?'

'I ate a lot. I think I'll be fine until tomorrow,' she replied.

'We'll see.'

They sat there for a while, reading. Anders leafed through one of Kati's coffee table books. Later they lay on top of the coverlet on her bed for several hours, talking. The same bubble formed around them, and the hours flew by as Anders told her about his family, about his crazy paternal grandfather, about the frequent hospital stays of his childhood, about his trip to Vietnam. Kati talked about food. She said that was her big passion.

'But I've totally lost inspiration when it comes to cooking right now. All I do is heat things up in the microwave or oven. But I can still talk about food and dream about it and fantasise about it. Or I can read recipes. I just don't feel like doing any cooking myself,' she said.

'Sometimes all you really want is mashed potatoes and meatballs with cream gravy,' said Anders.

'You're right,' said Kati. 'Meatballs and mashed potatoes would taste good right now.'

Around them the world teemed with life, and the air filled with a warm scent of pine needles and resin. They were walking towards the public beach, which was about two kilometres from the bay.

For the most part, Kati asked him about himself. She didn't say anything more about her own life, giving only vague answers when he asked any questions. Occasionally she would stop mid-sentence and change the subject, as if trying to avoid certain topics.

Anders had a feeling that their whole relationship was something temporary, but that didn't bother him.

It was almost – when he thought about it – as though she was spending time with him because it gave her something to do. As if he was a client, a way for her to practice her skills as a therapist.

The most important thing was being allowed to talk, to acknowledge the closeness that arose in their conversations.

'What are you going to do when autumn comes?' she asked.

'I don't really know,' he said. 'But for once it doesn't seem terrible that I don't know.'

'Will you go and stay with your parents? You don't have to answer that question. I'm just curious. It's an occupational habit of mine.'

'The situation is complicated. I have a complicated relationship with them.'

'That's more common than uncommon in most families,' she said.

'Sure, but I think … Oh, I don't know. But I think I might have been a happier person, more like other people, if I was interested in what people are generally interested in. I don't know when I got the way I am. I started reading philosophy in secondary school, and that shaped my world view. I adopted a pessimistic outlook. Sometimes I think it would be nice to have a girlfriend and watch TV in the evening and maybe start a family. But that doesn't seem on the cards for me. Instead, I went to Hanoi, chasing God knows what. Even I don't know what I was looking for. The whole trip was a complete waste of time.'

'But there are lots of people who go to Thailand and Vietnam and live there for a year or so, precisely because they have no idea what they're looking for.'

'I just want ... I don't know ...'

They both fell silent. He wondered if this was also part of her therapeutic methods, allowing the silence to speak.

'If you were working right now, it would be awfully expensive for me,' he said then.

'What do you mean?'

She was walking ahead of him along the narrow path, pushing aside branches that blocked the way.

'I mean, if you were my therapist.'

'Well, I work for the municipality, so it's not expensive. You just have to get a referral. Does it feel like I'm working when I talk to you?'

'I don't know. Maybe a little. Now and then.'

'That's not my intention,' she said. 'I enjoy your company. I really do.'

They arrived at the beach and spread their towels on one of the sand dunes higher up. Kati went to the bathing hut to change her clothes.

'Could you put some of this on me?' she asked when she came back. She handed him a tube of sunblock. She knelt down as he rubbed the lotion on her back. She was so thin that he could see the vertebrae under her skin, which was covered with freckles.

'What are those pills you have in your bag?' Kati asked him.

'Pills?'

'It's not that I've been snooping through your things. But when I got out my towel, I saw some pills in there.'

'Don't worry about them. I should throw them out.'

'But what are they for?'

'Just my medicine. I have Crohn's disease. It's an infection of the small intestine. I've had it all my life.'

'But the pill bottle doesn't look like it came from a chemist shop.'

'No, those pills are special. Just something I brought back from Hanoi.'

'Are they drugs?'

'I suppose you could say that.'

'Are they any good?'

'What do you mean?'

'I mean, do they produce a good effect?'

'Are you saying you want to try some?'

'I don't know.'

He looked at her as she lay face down on the towel. There was no sign that she'd been outdoors in the sun all summer, but she had a lovely olive-coloured skin that probably didn't burn very easily. He, on the other hand, burned bright red on his arms and face as soon as he got out in the sun.

He was so different from Kati. He could tell they'd been shaped by different experiences. It was possible that they actually had no common language. But then why did everything seem so easy when he was with her?

When he was a teenager, Anders got a serious glimpse of the social control that a small town exerts on its residents. He sometimes thought that Ekenäs might as well have been a medieval Catholic town when it came to how regulated everything was, how difficult it was to break with the norms, and how fiercely a person was punished for trying to do that. Maybe it seemed especially harsh because the town was so picturesque and in many ways idyllic – with the low wooden homes, the cobblestones and the open marketplaces. But when he was exposed to the local social life, he had a feeling he was in the exercise yard of a prison. Everyone seemed predestined to assume specific roles, and there was no chance of doing anything different. Maybe Ekenäs, in particular, was that way because it was so close to Helsinki, but with forest in between, as if it were cut off from the rest of the world. Hangö was the closest town, and it was even more extreme with its failing industries, its unemployment, its beautiful villas from a bygone era.

When Anders began secondary school, he felt as if he'd been tossed into a controlling system. As he dashed to a class – he was late because he couldn't find the room at first – an older student yelled after him: 'That boy is going to run himself to death.' The comment wasn't especially mean, but the way he said it was.

With secondary school came the entire arsenal of teenage shenanigans. Smoking behind the school building, in an area called the 'pit', where Anders soon ended up, even though his knees were practically shaking the first time he went there. The first taste of alcohol (Anders and his friends bought beer from a local man who was well known in town because he cycled every-where with big bags on his bicycle rack); and his first serious attempts with the opposite sex.

But also the sudden insight that the adult world was a sham, that everything the grown-ups claimed was false, and the harder they hammered home their viewpoints, the more they lied. All this in combination with the absurd hierarchies in Ekenäs social life, the harsh macho culture in which guys on mopeds still ruled during those last short years before they were left behind in the small town while others made their escape and created new lives for themselves. All this made Anders hate Ekenäs. He hated the small-town pettiness, he hated being a Finland-Swede and being born into this pathetic section of Finnish society, a member of the minority that was reputed to be snobbish but was really just inbred and stupid and in the best case harmlessly old-fashioned, but in the worst case a totally backward part of the world that would only get worse and worse the longer it existed.

But then there was Kati. And a completely different feeling. He lay down next to her and looked up at the sky. Not a cloud in sight.

'We could give it a try someday, if you want,' he said. 'There's nothing weird about the pills. They just make you feel good, and life seems simpler.'

'That sounds like something that would really suit me at the moment,' she said.

'It suits most people.'

He turned to look at her.

'Tell me more about your cooking.'

'Right now?' she said.

'Yes. Tell me how you make cream gravy.'

'Are you serious?'

'Yes. I don't know why, but it was so great hearing you talk about food earlier.'

She turned onto her back and squinted up at the sky. She placed a hand over her face.

'I usually avoid using wheat flour,' she said.

'Then what?'

'I usually make cream gravy with butter, mustard, bouillon and cream. It's very simple and very good.'

'Tell me more,' said Anders.

She laughed.

'Then I add a little Worcestershire sauce to the ground meat so the meatballs will have a slightly saltier taste.'

'What else?'

'Mashed potatoes. Butter and milk. And the potatoes should be as mealy as possible. That makes them soft and fluffy.'

Anders felt both safe and excited. Her voice was low and gentle and a bit hoarse.

'And lingonberry preserves?'

'Of course,' said Kati. 'And pickles, if there are any.'

'What else do you make?'

She laughed again. 'That's all!'

'But do you make other sorts of dishes? I want to hear more about what you cook.'

'Do you like food?' asked Kati.

'What do you think? Haven't you noticed what I look like? Tell me more.'

'I make cakes.'

'Yum. What kind of cakes?'

'Brita cake. It's a cream-filled layer cake with strawberries.'

'Oh.'

He turned towards her, leaned down, and kissed her. She hesitated at first, but then kissed him back. He could feel himself getting an erection, so he lay down on his stomach.

'How do you make a layer cake? Tell me all the details,' he said.

Again she laughed, turning over so he saw how the sand had stuck to her breasts.

Anders reluctantly went back to the summer house in the evening. Erik was sitting on the terrace, having a beer, and Anders nodded to him. Erik hastily stood up, wobbling a bit before heading for the steps.

'Where have you been?'

'Nowhere.'

'Nowhere? All day?'

Erik frowned before sitting back down, almost falling off his chair.

'It was such nice weather, and I thought I needed to be alone for a while.'

'Did you talk to anyone?'

'Me? No, I didn't.'

'Huh,' said Erik. He sounded sceptical. 'Are you sure about that?'

Anders thought Erik might have seen him with Kati. It was possible. Did it matter?

'And you didn't even bother to come home to have dinner with us,' said Erik.

'But I did. I'm here now.'

Erik looked as if he'd been drinking steadily all day. He gave Anders that sort of look: focused and yet restless, as if he was trying to formulate something scathing to say but couldn't find the right words. He did not look happy.

'Is there something you want to ask me?' said Anders as gently as possible.

'I don't want to ask you anything. I have no problems. You're the one who borrows money from me and comes here without saying how long you plan to stay, and then we hardly see you. You just hang around the beach with some woman you don't even know. Your generation seems to have no idea what it means to take responsibility or what it is you want.'

'My generation? You're only two years older than me. We're the same generation,' said Anders, sitting down next to Erik on the terrace.

'Are the two of you having sex?'

'Who do you mean?'

'You and Kati.'

'So you know her name?' said Anders. 'I don't know why you're asking me that, when it's none of your business. But no, we're not having sex. Mostly we talk about cooking.'

Erik stood up again, swayed, and went to the front door.

He stood there for a long moment, breathing as he stared at the ground. He reminded Anders of their paternal grandfather. Erik looked at least ten years older than his real age.

'Forget it. I just thought … you came here and … You haven't even asked me how I'm doing … Forget it.'

He opened the door and went inside.

2

ONE MORNING IN LATE JULY Julia found the family car down at the road, almost in the ditch. It must have rolled down there. As if the handbrake had failed. As if someone had been playing in the car and then let it roll away, across the road. Nothing had happened to the car. It was almost as if it had been parked at the drive leading to the big grey house where the melancholy woman lived. The woman Anders had started spending time with. The woman they knew nothing about. But the car hadn't been there the night before, and none of them had driven it anywhere.

Julia couldn't imagine the kids playing in the car. Anton wouldn't dare, and Alice wouldn't be interested in anything like that. When she asked Erik, he merely shrugged. He often sat on the terrace in the evenings, drinking. It seemed as if his plans to have a summer filled with activities like fishing and swimming had faded. Julia hadn't said anything to him because she didn't want to make him cross. But he'd already gone through a big bottle of Bacardi and two cases of beer.

'But don't you think it's a little strange? I mean, that the car would roll down there from the driveway? If I'd forgotten to set the handbrake, I think I would have noticed,' she said.

'Maybe you forgot after we came back from the grocery shopping,' Erik said. He had a beer in front of him, and he was eating a sandwich.

'But that's what I'm saying. If I forgot, the car would have rolled down right away. But it didn't.'

'Was there any damage?'

'Not that I could see.'

'Okay then. Next time you need to leave the car in gear so it won't roll anywhere.'

'I think I'll go see Marika and Chris,' she said, and left.

She walked down to the beach, squinting in the warm July sun.

Chris was sitting in a lotus position outside the yurt, totally focused on what he was reading. His chest was bare. When he saw Julia, he got up, and that's when she noticed Helena was there too. She was lying on a blanket next to Chris, sunbathing topless.

Julia wondered how old Helena was. Surely no more than twenty? She thought it was easy for such a young woman to latch onto a man because she could exploit her own youth. She was someone who didn't need to take responsibility for the attractive aura or sexual energy she radiated. If she flirted with Chris, it was basically his job not to encourage her.

Something told Julia that he didn't really care about such things.

'Would you like some coffee?' he asked.

'Sure, why not,' said Julia. 'Where's Marika?'

'I don't know. Around here somewhere. Wait, I remember now. She was going to town to shop for groceries,' he said, showing no interest in the subject.

The beach was deserted, and Julia couldn't see any of the others, except for Ville, who was sitting outside the house working on his laptop. Julia hadn't really talked to him. He had always kept in the background, something of a bit player among Chris's disciples.

She went over to Ville, wanting to ask him whether he'd seen the children. He too looked young, at least ten years younger than her. She thought he seemed like one of those young Finnish men who flocked to various extreme-right groups, like Soldiers of Odin or climate dystopia, creating a new context for themselves when society offered no prospects.

Ville was talking to somebody on Skype.

'Am I disturbing you?' she asked.

'I'm talking to a client, but it can wait,' he said, closing up his computer after ending the conversation.

Ville had told Erik that he came from Seinäjoki, but that's all she really knew about him. He had a scruffy beard and looked a bit dishevelled, but there was a certain warmth to his gaze.

'What sort of work do you do?'

'As little as possible,' he said. 'But you might say that I work on the fringes of the internet.'

'As a hacker?'

'That's not a word I'd use. As I see it, it's a matter of freedom of expression and freedom in general. And that's becoming more and more important in today's world.'

'Huh,' said Julia. 'Have you seen the children?'

'Whose children?'

'My daughter. And Leo.'

'Not for a couple of days,' said Ville. 'I don't really pay much attention to other people.'

Julia went back to Chris and Helena. Helena's light-brown skin looked so soft, and Julia found herself getting lost in a fantasy about pressing her finger against Helena's stomach, the way she might press her thumb into a stress ball. The young woman's arms looked pale against the dark sand, where several empty beer cans had been tossed.

Julia noticed how messy the yard was, as if no one had done

any cleaning in ages. In addition to the beer cans there were plastic sacks filled with rubbish, and cigarette butts and ice cream wrappers scattered about. A big rubber boat that someone had tried to inflate but then abandoned lay next to the yurt.

'Are Alice and Leo here?' she asked.

Alice had left early in the morning without saying a word to anyone, and she hadn't yet returned home. Julia had assumed the kids had gone down to the beach, but she didn't see them when she walked past.

'They're fine. Why don't you sit down?' said Chris.

'Okay,' said Julia as Chris smiled, feigning naïvity. During the summer she'd worked out what sort of person he was. She'd met his kind before. He was a man who'd made it far in life by smiling that way, yet on some level he knew there were also limits to using his charm as currency, especially having reached middle age. Men like that had a tendency to acquire younger girlfriends, since boyish charms didn't work on women their own age. Older women were much quicker to recognise his type, and they understood that there might not be much of substance beyond the first impression.

Poor Marika, thought Julia.

Chris handed her a cup of coffee.

'We're considering moving here,' he said now.

'Really?' said Julia.

'Yes. Putting down roots here, in fact. Maybe organising a large festival or workshop with people from all over the world. You should join us.'

For some inexplicable reason, Julia didn't go back home. She stayed there at the shore, listening to Chris as he told her about his plans for the movement while Helena sat close by, watching them with a look of deep concentration, as if she were trying to seduce Chris through telepathy.

Julia asked Helena whether she had a boyfriend. She couldn't resist breaking the mood. She wanted to see the young woman's reaction, rather like a child tearing the wings off a butterfly to see if it could still move.

But Helena did not seem surprised or taken aback.

'That's such a heteronormative question,' she said.

'What do you mean?'

'You assume I'd be with a man.'

'Okay. So, are you seeing anyone?'

'Now you sound like my paternal grandmother in Greece. Life doesn't have to be so binary. Did you know that? Although I suppose it is when you're married,' said Helena.

'Chris is married too,' said Julia.

Chris smiled again.

'Actually,' said Chris, 'Marika and I aren't married. Did you think we were?'

Julia glanced at his left hand.

'Oh, you mean this ring I'm wearing? It's a family heirloom. I've had it all my life,' he said, looking at the wide silver band he wore on his left ring finger.

He stood up and brushed off the sand.

'Anyone interested in a little dessert?'

'Sure,' said Helena.

It turned out that what Chris called 'dessert' was an electronic cigarette with marijuana. Julia declined since it was still morning and she didn't really care for the effect. The few times she'd smoked grass, she had felt jittery and restless.

After a while a mellow mood came over Chris and Helena, as if they were sinking into a lethargic state. The sun was so hot that Julia had to move into the shade.

Chris talked about how the human era was following the same pattern as Greek drama.

'And that's why civilisation is a tragedy, if we're going to classify it as a specific genre. All the horrors are pre-determined,' he said.

Helena lay with her head resting on his lap. She nodded at his statements with the same admiration a first-year college student might show whenever her philosophy professor said something brilliant. She glanced at Julia, her expression clearly saying: 'Don't come here and pretend you're anybody.'

'It's encoded in the human DNA, in the whole information process. The more technological advances we make, the closer we come to our own annihilation. It's like fireworks. Or like waves that break up under their own weight. We humans are too smart for our own good,' he said.

'That's awfully pessimistic,' said Julia. 'There are lots of movements that want to make the world better and more sensible.'

'Yes, but it doesn't matter what kind of political system we have. Capitalism, or a growth economy, is often seen as the villain in the drama, but where does it come from? Where does industrialisation come from? These days, it's all about civilisation. And that's the whole problem,' he went on.

'So when did the tragedy start, in your opinion? With the Big Bang? When human beings migrated from Africa?' asked Julia.

'From a purely technical standpoint, maybe when humans began eating fish and their brains developed so much that they could think more abstractly. That's when they began leaving traces in nature,' said Chris.

'So things were better before that?' asked Julia.

'That's right. Today's world is a sham.'

Helena seemed annoyed by Julia's questions, but Julia thought Chris was trying to impress her, and the more she looked at him and listened to his remarks, the more comical he seemed.

'The world is a sham?' she said now. 'That seems like a very grandiose statement.'

'People are always putting on an act, displaying a façade,' said Chris. 'And we keep getting better at doing that. There's a story about Goebbels and his lover, a Czech actress. Hitler demanded that he break off the relationship because it could cause a scandal. At the same time, those two men were killing six million Jews. I mean, how strange is that? Devoting lots of energy to make sure there are no stains on your personal reputation while committing the most horrific acts without even a trace of guilt. Civilisation is nothing but a thin veneer.'

Helena nodded as she ran her hand lightly over Chris's arm.

3

ERIK CREPT CLOSER TO Kati's house, wanting to peer in a window. He knew it was a childish thing to do, but he couldn't help it. He'd been drinking and now felt such a yearning, and yet he was so disappointed in himself. He should have pulled himself together and begun looking for a job; he should have done something about his situation, or at least spent some time with the kids. Instead, he merely sat on the terrace every evening, drinking rum and noticing how his muscles and his thoughts gradually relaxed until he sank into a pleasant torpor. Two big shots of rum were enough to make him drunk, but not too drunk. Just enough to smooth out any sharp edges.

There was no wind on this hot afternoon. Anders had gone down to the beach early in the morning, and by three Erik had poured his first drink. When they'd first arrived here, he'd mentally set five o'clock as an okay time to start drinking, but today after lunch he'd already started longing for some rum.

Yesterday he'd driven the car to the supermarket even though he'd been drinking. It was his job to do the grocery shopping, and he didn't want Julia to know that he'd started drinking so early in the day. So he'd gone to town, driving as cautiously as he could and hoping no one would stop him and ask him to take a breathalyser test. That would have been unlikely, since it was only two in the afternoon. At the supermarket he stood in one spot for a long time, unable to recall what he was supposed to buy. It took him two tries to remember everything on his shopping list. When he finally had all the groceries, he drove home as if in a dream and unpacked the grocery bags in the kitchen. He must have forgotten to set the handbrake. He couldn't remember, but in some mysterious way the car had rolled down to the road during the night.

He got closer to Kati's house, but he didn't hear any voices or laughter. In his mind he pictured what they were doing inside: his brother and Kati having sex. Anders' big, beefy body on top of her lovely dark silhouette. She would come several times while he spilled his seed onto her stomach. Why was he tormenting himself with these kinds of thoughts? He didn't know. He felt obsessed.

He sneaked behind the house to the front door, stopped a few metres from the terrace, and stared at the big window facing the bay. But the sun was reflecting off the glass, and he couldn't see anything. He thought they might catch sight of him; they definitely would if he went any closer. So instead he went around to the side of the house and peered in through a window. It was dark inside. He was looking at an empty room.

He thought: What am I doing here?

Someone opened the door to the room and came in. It was Kati. When Erik saw her, he quickly moved away from the window, but he wasn't fast enough. She saw him.

He fled.

As he ran towards the road he could hear his brother calling after him. Or maybe he just imagined he heard Anders' voice. Maybe it wasn't too late, maybe he could still save the situation. But by running away, he'd managed to emphasise how absurd it was, so all he could do now was continue heading for the road and home.

Erik was packing. Julia came back just as he was carrying his suitcase out to the terrace. He told her he was going to catch a train, and he could drive himself to the station if she didn't want to take him.

'You're going to Helsinki? Right now?' she asked.

'Yes. It's sort of an emergency. The whole department store is having trouble with the internet, and I can't fix it over the phone. I need to go back and have a look at the servers.'

'Okay,' she said. 'Maybe it'll do you good to go back to the city for a while. How long are you staying?'

'Probably just a few days.'

'All right. Shall I drive you to the station now?'

'In an hour. Let's leave at five.'

He didn't want Anders to turn up and force him to explain, so he went down to the cellar, giving the excuse that he wanted to have another look at the pipes and maybe find out where the strange smell was coming from. It was dark and damp under the house. The floor was cement, and an oil-fired boiler stood in one corner of the room. He looked at the pipes and realised he had no idea where to start.

There was water all over the floor, at least five centimetres deep. The water hadn't been there earlier in the summer.

He sat down on a stool and spent a little while surfing the internet on his mobile. He pictured how he would organise his life when he got back to Helsinki. How he'd pull himself together.

I'm basically a positive and optimistic person, he told himself now.

He'd been an important cog in the wheel at his job, and he still had a lot to offer the world.

He was a good person.

He was a smart person.

He was a good father and a good husband.

He was optimistic and happy.

He still had his best years ahead of him.

He was in good physical shape.

He was happy.

He was good at his job.

No one was better at his job.

He wondered if there was anyone he could call, someone on his phone list who might be helpful. The more he thought about this, the clearer it became that he was going to have to ring Martin.

He'd thought about doing that many times over the years. Martin owed him, and in spite of everything, they had a shared history. But until now there had never been any reason for Erik to get in touch with him.

He stood up with the water lapping at his shoes. The light from his phone lit up the room. He pulled up Martin's name and considered calling him, but then he stuck the phone back in his pocket.

Julia drove him to the train station. Erik had managed to avoid Anders, which wasn't that difficult. Anders had apparently moved in with Kati, and there was nothing Erik could do about it. As far as he could recall, his brother had never had a relationship that lasted long enough for his family to know about it. Anders had spent a year at the community college after finishing secondary school, then studied philosophy and something equally vague at the university in Helsinki. But if Erik were to be completely honest, he'd never been especially interested in what Anders did.

For a few years when they were kids, Erik and Anders had been best friends. Erik thought back to one of the family trips to Spain. He was ten, Anders was eight. He pictured Anders holding a lizard in his hand. Anders high up on a boulder. Anders spending hours out in the water with a snorkel. Their paternal grandparents were there too. Grandma floating in the sea in the daytime, or at least that's how Erik remembered her – floating easily because it was saltwater. He pictured the gold chain around Grandpa's tanned neck, his shirt unbuttoned. He recalled the calamari and ketchup – Erik and Anders ate the same thing every night.

They stayed in two flats: his family in one, his grandparents in the other. And even though Anders was younger, he used to climb over the balconies between the two flats, completely unafraid, until one day the hotel owner saw him. The man stood on the ground below and shook his fist as he shouted. From then on they all called him the 'no-more-balcony-climbing man.' When their grandfather heard about it, he flew at Anders in a rage, chasing him down the hotel corridor while Erik stood outside their door, terrified. The gold chain clinked when Grandpa took off after Anders, but Erik couldn't see even a trace of fear in his brother's eyes. All he saw was a glint of awe at the sequence of events he'd caused. Erik, on the other hand, was so scared that he rushed to the door of their flat, and when he tried to open it, he turned the key so fast that it broke off in the lock. He almost pissed himself. The fact that he'd broken the key was suddenly much worse than climbing from one balcony to the other, and his grandfather grabbed Erik by the ear – at least this was how he remembered it – and dragged him out of the hotel down to the pool where the others were sitting. It hurt terribly, and the pain in his ear lasted for several days afterwards.

The family directed their fury at Erik for the rest of the day. Anders gave him a nod and said 'thanks' when they were having dinner in the hotel restaurant, eating calamari of course.

Erik thought about all this as he sat in the train drinking the beer he had ordered. Anders had never had any sense of responsibility; he'd always taken the world for granted, always treated life as a joke.

Erik got out his mobile and rang Martin. A female voice told him the phone number was no longer in use. He opened his laptop and looked through his email until he found Martin's name. He typed a few lines and hoped for the best.

4

ALICE AND LEO HAD agreed to meet in the woods that morning, in the same place where they'd found the dead moose. They'd decided it was now their place, filled with a mystique and significance that only they understood.

Neither of them had slept the previous night, since they'd spent the whole time chatting online. Leo wrote that his parents had changed their minds. They no longer wanted to stay in Mjölkviken, as they'd initially planned. He wrote in a mixture of English and Swedish, exactly the way so many of Alice's friends did. And even though they didn't write about anything important, just sent each other various gifs and YouTube videos, Alice felt close to Leo, as if they were communicating in the same language, with the same humour and the same sarcasm. It was Leo who finally made the suggestion:

Leo: Have you thought about something
Alice: What
Leo: That we could meet instead of lying here with our phones
Alice: True
Alice: Where should we meet?
Leo: The moose?
Alice: Do you remember where it was?
Leo: Yup

Alice: Now?
Leo: Ten minutes
Alice: OK

It started to rain after Alice left. It was so quiet in the woods she could hear the first raindrops falling; it felt as if the trees were coming to life all around her.

She had to wait a while for Leo. She sought shelter under a spruce, sitting on the warm moss and leaning against the tree trunk. Soon the rain surrounded her like a symphony. It was still hot, with a low pressure system. Heat rose from the ground, steam issuing from the moss.

Alice wasn't stupid. She was well aware that this whole situation was temporary, that she should be grateful that the summer had provided her something that would make her stand out. She and Leo might have very little contact with each other when their schools began, and gradually they would lose even that contact. That was just fine.

Yet, as she waited for him, it felt like there was something more to this. Something in the air, as if she were catching a glimpse of how it might feel to be in love for real, to be happy to see someone.

And there he was, walking towards her in the rain, wearing rubber boots and a raincoat. She felt her cheeks tighten as she gave him her biggest smile.

'Hi,' he said.

'Hi,' she said.

'What is it?' he asked.

'I don't know. You just look so cute.'

Leo rolled his eyes and sat down.

'Cosy place you've found here,' he said.

'I know. Right?' said Alice, smiling. She was bubbling over inside.

'Do you remember when you were little playing hide-and-seek and you always had your own special place that nobody else knew about?'

'I don't know. We never played hide-and-seek in Helsinki. Maybe once at school.'

Leo laughed. 'You've never played hide-and-seek?'

'Never.'

'Well, then you've missed out on a lot. Want to play now?'

'Now?'

'You can hide first.'

'For real?' asked Alice.

'It might be fun.'

'I'd rather stay here,' she said.

'Okay, then I'll hide. You have to count to a hundred.'

Leo stood up before Alice could object. She stayed seated under the spruce, half-heartedly closing her eyes since she wasn't sure whether Leo was serious. She didn't want to start counting and then feel stupid when he said he was just kidding.

But she heard him moving further away, with twigs snapping under his feet. Alice sat there in the rain, staring straight ahead. She felt as though she was in a movie, as if the rain were leaving scratches on an old type of film because it was falling so evenly. She thought about something she'd read in school, that the ground water was formed when water seeps into the ground, that it takes place so slowly that all bacteria and pollutants were filtered out, and that's why it was possible to drink it. The water could be close to a thousand years old. Somehow that seemed so wonderful. She was thirsty just thinking about it. She leaned forward from under the spruce and stuck out her tongue. The rain tasted so good.

She was all alone in the woods now. Leo was no longer anywhere in sight. She was suddenly aware of her solitude, and it felt a bit eerie. She stood up to see where he might have gone, guessing he would have headed towards the sea, so she followed the path that led down to the road.

She walked ten metres or so but then hesitated. Could he really have gone this far? It seemed like a silly game, and she could see why she'd never played hide-and-seek before. She couldn't see him anywhere, nor was there any place he could be hiding. The pines were set far apart and quite slender, so he couldn't hide behind them. She went over to a small boulder and peeked behind it, but he wasn't there. She paused and leaned against the rocks as she got out her mobile to check for coverage.

She had only a little battery left.

Alice: This is a stupid game

Leo didn't answer. He didn't seem to have noticed her text. She sat down on the rock and began using up the rest of her battery surfing on the internet.

'Leo?' she called timidly.

'Leo!' she shouted.

She considered going back home. If Leo thought this was fun, he could stay out here and have fun by himself. She wasn't interested.

All of a sudden a text appeared on her mobile.

Leo: Look behind you

Alice turned around. There he stood, his golden hair completely soaked, with a big smile on his face and a black cloth bag in his hand. She read what it said on the bag: FEMINIST.

'I'm sorry,' said Leo. 'It was supposed to be a surprise. I ran home to fetch some breakfast for us. I thought we could find a good place to sit. You don't have to go home, do you?'

'No,' said Alice. She didn't need to go home.

They went to the root cellar by the tennis courts and ate their food in the light of the bare bulb. It didn't matter that the cellar was damp and smelled of mould, it was still romantic.

Afterwards, they kissed for a long time. Alice had never felt anything like this before. She'd never done any serious kissing. Now she ran the tip of her tongue over his lips and tasted him.

He wanted her to touch him down there, so she did, but she didn't want him to do the same thing to her; it felt too private. Yet she felt safe with him, as if there was nothing to worry about. He asked if he could touch her breasts, and she let him do that. She wanted him to, it felt good, it tickled when his fingertips touched her nipples.

Afterwards Leo told her that he thought his family would be leaving soon.

'Already? But the summer isn't over yet. We still have several weeks left,' said Alice.

'It's always like this. My parents start arguing, and it's usually about some of Pappa's friends, and then I know what will happen. The next step is they leave for some new place where they gradually gather new people around them in new chapters,' he said. 'I'm so fucking tired of all that.'

Alice wondered if this meant that Leo always met girls at different places, and then he had to say goodbye to them.

'Do you think we'll ever see each other again?' she asked.

'Fuck if I know. This morning Mamma said we're going to sell this place. A few days ago, they said we were moving here. I can't make any sense out of them.'

'We need to stay in contact,' said Alice.

'Let's forget about all that for now. What would you like to do?'

'I don't know.'

He leaned forward and kissed her on the mouth, lightly but so slowly that she tasted the salt on his lips.

'You know what we should do?' he said.

'What?'

'We should run away. At least temporarily. Just for one night.'

'Where would we go?' asked Alice. She had already decided to say yes. She couldn't think of anything else she would rather do. To get away from the subdued anger of the summer house, to do something besides lying on the rocks, staring at her phone and listening to music and waiting for something to happen in her life.

'There are lots of places around here. There's a campsite not far away, maybe a couple of kilometres. Maybe we could break into a cabin. Or we could just sleep on the beach.'

'In the rain?'

'Why not?'

5

'HEY MAN, SIT DOWN. Do you want a beer?'

It was only noon, but Erik realised that over the course of the summer he'd become a person who drank beer even at lunch. He'd awakened this morning, back home in their Helsinki flat, and decided to do whatever he felt like doing today.

But as soon as he'd finished breakfast, he'd received an email from Martin, and they'd agreed to meet in the city.

They hadn't seen each other in a long time. Maybe two or three years. Erik – like most Finns – had seen Martin in interviews in various business magazines. A month ago a reporter for *Ilta-Sanomat* had phoned to ask Erik about the years he and Martin had studied together because he was writing an article about pioneers within the Finnish mobile phone industry.

'So what's happening on the career front for you? Have you made your first million yet?' asked Martin now.

He'd grown a beard, like every man over the past few years. But Martin always went one step further; he had a long, thick Jesus beard that somehow actually suited him.

'No, no million yet,' said Erik as he sat down.

'But you're the real winner,' said Martin.

'What do you mean?'

'Your kids are nearly teenagers. And you've got a beautiful wife.'

'Oh, sure. I suppose that's something,' said Erik.

Martin smiled. It was the same smile he'd had when they first met. Back then it had been the charming, idealistic smile of a fellow student. Now it had been transformed into the grin of a successful businessman.

Erik remembered how he'd loved the damp weather of Helsinki during that first autumn when he'd started at the University of Technology. He'd enjoyed hearing lecturers talk about the future, and how their school was a 'springboard for innovation', along with everything else that was discussed at the university in the early years of the twenty-first century. The main building – part of the campus designed by the famed Finnish architect Alvar Aalto in the 1950s – was a red brick structure surrounded by slender pines, with a boldly curved auditorium in the centre.

There were student associations, unlicensed booze shops and traditions that everyone was expected to follow after only a couple of weeks.

Like most of his fellow students, Erik lived in a tiny dorm room and shared a kitchen, which always smelled of greasy pizza boxes or some type of simmering meat dish. A boy from Nigeria named Obe lived on Erik's corridor, and he was always making big pots of stew that he would then freeze. The worktop was often covered with dirty casserole dishes.

It was obvious that the University of Technology was primarily a school for men.

'The only girls here are studying architecture,' Martin had said during a picnic in the rain in Gamla Kyrkan park. They'd partied the night before at an unlicensed booze shop near the Hanken School of Economics, sitting outdoors in the freezing cold. A group of ten or fifteen students, and not a single female.

Boozy picnics were a tradition. They drank schnapps and cooked sausages on a portable grill. The important thing was that nobody complained about the cold.

'Without the parties at Hanken, none of us would ever see any chicks at all. It'd be like a long, sad episode of *Star Trek*, with uglier suits,' said Martin.

That was true. The main reason for organising parties with the students at the School of Economics was to increase the female 'number count'.

That all seemed so far away now. In front of Erik sat a thirty-five-year-old millionaire who was famous all over Finland. A man who seized every opportunity to talk about how important the Finnish school system had been for his career, and who said he was more than happy to pay taxes. He also frequently talked about how he'd been raised by a single mother. He had created an entire narrative about himself, and the media loved to repeat it. Erik would not be surprised if one day somebody made a film about Martin's life. But who would play Erik, the failed sidekick who could have become a millionaire too, if only he hadn't been so cowardly and conservative?

'Can I offer you anything to drink?' asked Martin.

'What are you having?' asked Erik.

'Some sort of IPA. To be honest, it tastes like lukewarm piss. I'm thinking of ordering a Karhu beer. It's crazy what people are willing to drink just because it's called a microbrew.'

'I'll get a Karhu for both of us,' said Erik.

He couldn't say that he'd arranged to meet with Martin in order to ask for a job. At least not yet. He was hoping the subject would naturally come up in the conversation. Maybe Martin would ask him how things were going at the department store and that could segue into Martin mentioning that he needed someone reliable at his company.

Erik took a sip of his beer and looked out at the city. It was a Tuesday, so the streets were relatively quiet. Most Helsinki residents were still on holiday out in the country.

'So how's it going with … Liisa? Wasn't that her name?' he asked now.

Erik pretended not to recall her name, though of course he did. She had been Martin's girlfriend when they last saw each other several years ago. A beautiful, friendly, and intelligent woman. Yet another reason for him to be jealous. What was he really doing here? Hadn't he left that whole chapter behind?

'Oh, fuck. We broke up after a few months. And actually …' said Martin, raising his left hand to show off the smooth gold band on his ring finger.

'Oh, I see. Congratulations,' said Erik. 'Do I know her?'

'No, you don't. She's not from Finland.'

'Where did you two meet?'

'In Moscow, as a matter of fact. She's Russian. Yeah, I know what you're thinking. But it's not like that.'

'What do you think I'm thinking?' asked Erik.

'You're thinking the same thing all Finns do. Finnish man, Russian mail-order wife. But she's an attorney, her family has money, and she didn't have to marry me. And besides, that's not the point.'

'I think it sounds exciting … er, I mean, nice that you're married. Where do you live?'

'On Högbergsgatan. We have a child too.'

'Oh? I haven't read anything about that.'

'It all happened pretty fast. A little girl. So now Tanya is home most days. But we're thinking about moving. The climate here is so bloody cold. And the anti-Russian sentiment … well, fuck, I didn't realise it was so bad until I met Tanya. People stare at us in the city, as if they're afraid we're going to eat their children.'

'Really?'

'Well, not everybody. But it does happen. I can't understand how they can tell Tanya is Russian. But I suppose it's because she speaks Russian to our daughter.'

'Where are you thinking of moving?'

Erik finished his beer. It occurred to him that Martin had changed, after all. He looked heavier. It wasn't hard to picture him pushing a pram through the city. A large, prosperous man in his prime who always ate well – probably having Sunday dinners at some expensive restaurant in the southern part of the city.

'We've thought about Abu Dhabi. These days they have schools with Finnish curricula. So it would be the same education for the children, but super modern, and a better climate.'

'Huh, that sounds good.'

'Maybe just for a year or two. Right now Finland feels so cold,' he said.

Erik paused for a moment. He thought: it's so easy when you have money. That makes all sorts of opportunities available.

'But I think Helsinki has gotten better,' he said then.

'Think so?'

'The city seems more modern than when I moved here from Ekenäs. There are lots of people doing all sorts of creative things. And new cafés where we live.'

Martin shrugged.

'When you live in a society that is service-based and there's no real industry except for tourism, then you know things are bad. This country can't be saved by a few fucking freelancers eating brunch every day. Or by someone creating an app for take-away meals. I think Finland is going to hell, to be honest. And large parts of the population are so afraid of foreigners that we're never going to be a modern country. If you compare us to Sweden, for instance.'

Erik nodded.

For a few moments neither of them spoke, as if they'd already exhausted everything they had to say to each other.

'We had fun, all the same,' said Martin.

'We?'

'You and I, back when we were at university. I was thinking about that when I got your email. Do you remember that basement place we had in Kronohagen?'

'Of course I do,' said Erik.

During their second year at university, they had leased space in the basement of an old building on Estnäsgatan, having decided to open an internet company. They purchased two space heaters and brought in several tables they'd found at a flea market. They rigged up a coffee maker and a microwave and began making their plans.

When the first snow arrived that winter, they hardly even noticed. The place smelled of damp brick and wet rag rugs, and on certain days it was so cold that they couldn't keep the chill out of the room. It would seep in along the floor and settle in the brick walls. But they were so focused on what they were doing that they would go out only if they needed food or booze.

'We drank an awful lot,' said Erik.

'It was the perfect life. Earning a little money by making websites for Finland-Swedish institutions and drinking beer all day long,' said Martin.

'You were a Marxist back then,' said Erik.

'I still am. Have you read anything by Thomas Piketty?'

'No, I haven't.'

'You should. It turns out that Lenin was right. And the worst part is that the concentration of capital just keeps rising. We thought we'd abandoned that system, but in reality it's just getting worse. Never before in the history of humankind have so few owned so much.'

'The job market seems very uncertain these days,' said Erik.

'So, where are you working?' asked Martin.

'I used to work there,' he said, pointing to the department store across the street.

Martin looked at him in surprise. 'Things aren't going so well at the store, from what I've read.'

'No, that's why I left.'

'What are you going to do now?'

'I don't know. Do you have any suggestions?'

Martin looked over at the bar without answering. 'Would you like another beer?' he asked, holding up his empty glass.

Erik left the pub with a feeling of despair that was even worse than during the train ride to Helsinki. 'I'll be in touch,' was the last thing Martin had said when they parted, but it was the sort of remark people make when they really have no intention of getting in touch again. Martin had explained – in great detail, which wasn't like him – that his company was going to be forced to restructure. ('But please don't tell anyone. We don't want the news to reach the media yet.') Apparently they'd been hiring far too many employees lately.

Erik walked along Esplanaden, heading for the Salutorget marketplace. He felt old. Was it possible to have a midlife crisis at the age of thirty-seven? Apparently it was.

He decided to go to Kapellet and have another beer. He needed time to think. When he stood at the bar and placed his order, he picked up a newspaper and sat down to leaf through it. When he came to page 20, he suddenly saw a familiar face. It was the article written by the reporter who had interviewed him earlier in the summer:

FINLAND'S LEFTIST START-UP MILLIONAIRE IS HAPPY TO PAY TAXES

Only ten years ago, Finland's famed IT millionaire Martin Westerlund was still living in his childhood home. Today he has bought a luxury house for his mother, and his fans include Nobel Prize winners. But he's not thinking of leaving Finland.

'I want to give something back to society.'

'Can't go to bed. Must. Catch. More. Zombies.'

That's what Paul Krugman, the Nobel Prize winner in economics, tweeted at the end of March. He is not the only one who has recently discovered the addictive Finnish mobile game Zombieswap. Basically it's about building up small societies of zombies as a work force. Zombieswap has topped the list of the most downloaded games on iTunes for fourteen months in a row.

It's hard to say what creates a successful mobile game. In the case of Zombieswap, it seems to be a combination of many things: the relatively simple graphics that bring to mind the 8-bit games of the 80s; the endless possibilities the game offers for building your own world as big as you want; the cute characters; the ironic criticism of society that particularly resonates with older players.

The game's chief designer and Dooku co-founder, Martin Westerlund, is known to be a big fan of George Romero's old zombie films, and he wanted to make use of the films' allegorical messages. In Zombieswap, you can use your own zombies to harvest digital crops or work in a factory, but they can also rebel.

'In a way it's a microcosm of the capitalist system, at least the way it used to be. The more malcontent the zombies are, the more difficult the game is to play. But it's expensive to keep the zombies happy, and so the profit margins decrease. Maybe the political aspect is why Krugman is a fan,' said Westerlund when we meet at his large home in central Helsinki.

Earlier in the year Westerlund purchased a spacious flat (240 square metres), which he is now remodelling. In the courtyard is his latest purchase, a Toyota 2000GT from 1969.

'The same car James Bond drives in *You Only Live Twice*. It's not as well known as the Aston Martins. But this is only the third car I've ever bought, so it's not about excessive purchases.'

Westerlund is married to the former Russian model Tatyana Ivanova. The couple have one child, with another on the way. Westerlund hired an architect to design the family home so he would have a separate section for himself. Not even his family members are allowed to enter. That may seem asocial, but Westerlund insists it's necessary.

'This is where I work, answer email, do interviews and keep my Playstation. I communicate with the rest of my family via an intercom system that is wired to the whole flat. I can be a significantly better father if I'm allowed to have time to myself,' he says.

When this reporter asks him if it wouldn't be easier to use a mobile phone instead of an intercom system, Westerlund surprisingly replies that he doesn't own a mobile.

'I've had intercom phones installed in the whole flat. I don't like being connected at all times. It's distracting and not good for the brain or the memory. I just use email, which I check sporadically,' he says.

This is only one of the many paradoxes about Westerlund. He's known for being eccentric and taking unexpected actions – such as his support for Finland's political party Left Alliance, contributing large sums of money prior to the latest parliamentary election. Westerlund is a supporter of government-funded health care, schools, etc., and he doesn't agree with privatisation or deregulation.

'I view Finland's education system as our greatest competitive advantage, and I think it will be even more important in the future. I detest populism and the intellectual sloppiness of our day, as well as the anti-science attitude that is rapidly gaining support,' he says.

One explanation for this may be Westerlund's own background. He was raised by a single mother who worked as a pre-school teacher and was active in the Social Democratic party on a local level.

'She is still working. Mamma won't retire until next year,' he says.

She won't exactly need to worry about her pension. Westerlund has bought her a luxury home not far from his own place.

'For a long time Mamma was concerned because all I did was sit at home writing code and taking apart old computers. She probably thought there was no hope for me. I doubt she thought it would ever lead to a real job. But she allowed me to continue, and I'm very glad she did.'

His father disappeared from the scene before he was born.

'We have no relationship,' says the millionaire, who clearly does not want to talk about his father. But Finnish media sources have revealed that his father is an entrepreneur who lives in Helsinki with his wife and children.

'I have no comment,' Westerlund says when asked.

Westerlund has not transferred any of Dooku's profits to foreign banks. And when the company goes public in the near future, the board of directors will remain in Helsinki.

'We often see how this type of business moves too fast and squanders money on expensive marketing campaigns. I think our brand is strong enough without making use of PR ploys such as stuffed animals, school backpacks and soft drinks,' he says.

The company was founded in the early 2000s when

Westerlund was still living at home with his mother. Of the two founders, only Westerlund remains part of the company.

'I was the only one who believed in it. But we made a lot of mistakes in the beginning, and the market wasn't ready for us. Lately I've had tremendous luck,' he says.

Dooku has already been called 'the next Nokia', but Westerlund dismisses such comparisons.

'We have only sixty employees and will never hire as many people as Nokia did, which was in the thousands.'

The other founder of Dooku was Erik Holmberg, who met Westerlund at the University of Technology when they were both students. They started their own company and began making websites for smaller enterprises, operating out of a cramped basement space in the trendy Kronohagen district of Helsinki.

'If I worked eight hours a day, Martin would work sixteen. He was always two steps ahead of me,' says Erik Holmberg today as he recalls those early years.

It's unclear what caused Holmberg to leave the company, but he assures me it had nothing to do with any personal differences.

'I became a father and wanted a more stable lifestyle. Back then we were hardly making any money,' he says.

Holmberg sold his shares in the company. If he hadn't done so, he would be a rich man today.

'Of course it may seem like that was a foolish thing to do, but back then it seemed like a sensible decision, and it does me no good to fret about it,' he says today.

After barely half an hour, Westerlund stops the interview.

'We have to go to the kitchen,' he says.

It turns out that his whole family is waiting for us.

'We always have lunch together – it's sacrosanct,' remarks Westerlund.

His wife, Tatyana Ivanova, has made sandwiches and a small salad. She is dressed entirely in white, the same colour as the family's kitchen. The couple's two-year-old daughter joins us at the table, looking through a picture book.

'We don't let her have access to any computers or kids' records,' says Ivanova. 'Research shows that they inhibit a child's development. And as often as possible, we let her run around and play outside in Brunnsparken.

'I grew up in the middle of Moscow, with all the concrete and traffic. It's liberating to live in Helsinki. It's a smaller city, and I don't lack for anything.'

That's not so strange. According to rumours, a large Japanese investor is interested in acquiring a majority share after the company goes public. The market value for the entire company is estimated at 10 billion euros.

'Right now we have no plans to sell our share, but the future will determine what direction we take,' says Westerlund.

At the time of the interview, Erik hadn't realised it would be such a long article. The reporter had phoned, and he'd quickly answered a few questions. It seemed dishonest that none of the company's problems were discussed in the article. The same old narrative about Martin Westerlund was repeated because no one wanted to hear about yet another Finnish company having financial troubles. Everybody wanted to believe that start-ups would pull Finland out of its economic depression, and that was why this type of interview barely scratched the surface instead of presenting any in-depth financial journalism.

Sooner or later the news would get out, of course. People

would see that the emperor had no clothes on, and then the journalists would seize every opportunity to trounce Martin. But for now, he was allowed to play the role of the beneficent millionaire with the social democratic heart.

Erik wandered aimlessly around town for several hours, moving from one pub to another. He didn't see anyone he knew. Everyone looked so young, mostly in their twenties, and they were constantly glancing at their phones, no matter who they were with.

He found a table in a quiet corner of a bar on Nylandsgatan and sat there for a long time, ordering beer after beer and staring at the display on his phone.

Julia rang just as he was thinking he ought to head back to the flat. She told him that Alice hadn't been home all day. 'I'm worried,' she said.

'What time is it, actually?' asked Erik.

'It's almost ten. She's been gone all day. She had already left by the time I got up this morning. And Marika and Chris haven't seen Leo either.'

'They've probably run away from home,' said Erik.

'Great. Should we call the police?'

'Why don't you try calling them first?'

'Her phone seems to be switched off. I haven't been able to reach her all day.'

'Nothing's going to happen.'

'Have you been drinking?' she asked.

'Just a few beers.'

'Right. So what should I do?'

'Nothing. This is Mjölkviken we're talking about. It's the safest place in the world,' said Erik.

6

JULIA AND MARIKA SPENT the whole evening searching for the kids. They walked back and forth along the shore and drove around the area several times, but eventually they had to give up. Anders had also helped out, searching in the woods for a few hours, but without finding any trace of Alice and Leo.

They told themselves that the kids must have gone down to the beach and taken a long walk, forgetting all about the time. So they went back to the summer house to make dinner. It had rained steadily during the day, a monotonous but persistent rain that made Julia feel even more worried. Surely the kids wouldn't voluntarily stay out in this kind of weather.

She cast an anxious glance at the clock. It was already ten thirty.

'You'd think they'd come home when they got hungry,' she said.

'Don't worry. Leo knows what he's doing,' said Marika.

'What do you mean by that?'

Julia wanted to ask Marika bluntly whether her son was a potential rapist, but since Anton was present, she restrained herself. Worry crept over her, and she had a hard time sitting still. She had an urge to ring the police, but the next second she decided the kids were bound to turn up on their own, so maybe she should wait another hour. And besides, what could the police do?

'I think all of us should go out and look for them,' said Julia. 'Chris, Helena, Ville, everybody.'

'I don't think Chris would agree to that,' said Marika.

Julia wanted to ask why, but intuitively she knew the answer. No doubt Chris's unconventional views also meant that children didn't need any rules or geographical limitations.

Marika tried to reassure Julia.

'We've always let Leo come and go pretty much as he pleases. He's used to being out in nature. He's grown up that way. Maybe the kids mentioned something to us this morning, but we didn't pay attention. Maybe we didn't really hear them.'

Julia wondered whether Marika condoned Chris's behaviour, whether the two of them had agreed that Chris and Helena could do whatever they wanted, and that their son could do whatever he wanted, so that one day he'd be like his father; maybe there were no rules whatsoever. Suddenly the behaviour of that whole family seemed so sordid, as if they had no boundaries. Why had she allowed Alice to be roped into their world? She felt guilty about thinking badly of Erik when she should have been happy that she had such a good, secure life, and that her husband was so normal.

'I get it that you don't have any rules, but I'm not used to letting my daughter run off without telling me where she's going,' said Julia.

'What time is she supposed to be home?' asked Marika.

'That's not what I mean,' said Julia. 'I wasn't expecting her to be running around at night in Mjölkviken. I didn't think I needed to give her a specific time to come home.'

'Nothing has happened to them,' said Marika. 'I promise you that. Even if they got lost in the woods, sooner or later they'll find their way back to the road because it's not that far away. I think that's most likely what happened.'

'But shouldn't we get the others to help us look for them?'

Marika glanced out of the window without saying anything for a moment. She no longer had her usual superior smile. 'Chris is down there with Helena. She turns up in the morning, and then they go off together. Or else she eats lunch with us, and it feels so horrible that she's still my friend when she looks at Chris like that, and … Well, it's not the first time.'

Julia turned to Anton. 'Maybe *you* should go out and look for them,' she told him.

'Now?' asked Anton.

'It's late, but it's still light out. Why don't you walk down to the road to see if they're on their way back.'

Anton reluctantly got up from the table. He picked up his mobile and went out the front door. Julia could see him through the window as he walked around outside the house, holding his phone in his hand.

'It's not as if this is anything new,' said Marika. 'Chris has always been like this. There have been lots of women. Young women.'

'Doesn't that bother you?' asked Julia, glancing at the clock again. It was ten forty. At eleven she was planning to take another walk along the beach.

'Maybe in the beginning … But by now I'm used to it.'

Julia didn't really know what to say. She was having a hard time concentrating on the conversation. She wanted to go out to look for the kids, go out and shout their names.

'Sometimes I think I should leave Chris. You know, just take Leo and go off somewhere. But where would I go? I've always thought that we could come here, but now he's claimed this place for himself too. Mjölkviken was the last place that was all my own. And now it feels like he's here with Helena and not with me.'

Julia could no longer keep her mind on what Marika was saying.

'I'm sorry, it sounds really awful. But right now I need to go out and look for the kids.'

'Again?'

'Yes.'

'I promise you, they're fine. They'll come back eventually,' said Marika.

'But I feel so helpless. I can't even phone them.'

'Think about when we were kids. Nobody had mobile phones to call each other. And everything went just fine.'

'I know, but I really want to get hold of them. Could you try phoning Leo again?'

They both tried, but neither of them got through. So they decided to go out again and look for the kids at the beach.

Marika kept on talking as they walked along in the rain. Anton went with them, carrying his mobile and lighting the way. Julia listened with only half an ear to what Marika was telling her. Occasionally she shouted for Alice and Leo. She felt like she'd ended up in some sort of therapy session with Marika, even though they both should have been focusing on finding the children.

'I've devoted such a big part of my life to distancing myself from my parents' way of life,' said Marika. 'Everything had to be so neat and tidy, with cocktails at five o'clock and a father who read the newspaper; friends with good taste, pearl necklaces, and children who played the piano. I've rebelled against all that and given Leo a free upbringing. And I've never owned even a single pair of earrings. I didn't want to be like my mother, who always agreed with everything Pappa said. Mrs Segerkvist, the doctor's wife, member of the local Odd Fellow club and loyal supporter of the Swedish People's Party in Finland. But when I look at my own life, I realise that I'm exactly the same. Chris is a leader who needs followers, and I'm the perfect trophy wife in his dream of an alternative lifestyle. I'm the Big Guru's personal PR assistant. That's what my life has become. Just like my mother's.'

Julia was a little surprised to hear all this. It wasn't what she'd expected. She had almost felt jealous of the relationship that Chris and Marika had, the sense that they were an adult couple who shared an adult relationship, emanating a sexual and slightly reckless tension that was neither conventional nor proper.

'My father was always drunk,' Marika went on. 'Always. I didn't really think about it back then. That's just the way he was. But your parents must have thought my father was hopeless. They were so smart.'

'I don't know about that,' said Julia.

'We've never talked about it,' said Marika.

'About what?' asked Julia.

'You wrote about it in your book. But you had no idea what it was really like.'

'You've read my book?'

Marika stopped and looked at Julia. 'Of course I've read your book. You wrote all about me and how annoying I was. And you're right. I was annoying. I wanted to spend every day with you; I couldn't bear the thought of not being with you. I was in love with you, or at least I thought I was. I couldn't do anything without you. But you thought I was trying to manipulate you.'

'Let's just forget it. None of that matters any more. We were so young.'

'I know, but in some way it was also very real. As if life were happening at that particular moment, and whatever happened was incredibly important. I remember that each day, each change, seemed like a matter of life or death. Each change. But you saw things differently. Although you didn't see everything.'

'What do you mean?' asked Julia.

'In your book you write that your childhood was like a shimmering, eternal summer, with late-night celebrations and parents who were happy and fun. There were firework displays at the end of the summer and crayfish parties and secret walks through the woods. The only thing that bothered you was me. I'm the worst thing in your book, your constant companion but also a constant torment. But you only saw what you wanted to see,' said Marika.

'What should I have seen?'

'Nothing. It's nothing.'

Marika's eyes suddenly lost some of the joy that usually made her look amused. 'Do you remember our parents ever telling us when we should go to bed?' she asked.

'No, never,' said Julia.

'Me neither. I can't recall that there were any rules.'

'Should we phone the police?'

'What is it you think the kids might be doing?' asked Marika.

'What did you do when you were thirteen?' replied Julia.

'Good Lord,' said Marika.

'Exactly.'

They both started laughing at the same time, and Marika put her hand on Julia's shoulder. Julia didn't shrug it off immediately. It felt reassuring in the midst of all this anxiety. Her shoulders were wet with rain. Then she deliberately moved forward, and they kept walking along the shoreline.

Marika lowered her voice. 'Do you remember the parties the grown-ups had, and how they acted when it was well past midnight?'

Julia thought back. She recalled her parents sitting in the patio chairs at Marika's house. She remembered how the children were seated at a different table. She remembered Mjölkviken in the autumn when it was already getting colder and darker. She remembered itchy socks and having to put on warmer clothes.

'What do you mean?' she asked.

'Do you remember all the fathers sticking their hands under

the mothers' shirts? And I don't mean their own wife's shirt. I mean the shirts of other women.'

'No, I don't,' said Julia.

'All of that went on. Maybe it wasn't the worst thing in the world. It was the 1980s, after all, and God knows things like that are still going on. But don't you remember that my father and your mother had something special?'

'No, I don't remember that,' said Julia.

'Well, they did. And there was a big ruckus one summer, and my mother took off. All I remember was that Pappa was drunk, as usual, and he hit her. And your mother came over, and she comforted him when my mother left, and I don't know how it happened, but your mother was still there the next morning.'

'What time is it?' Julia asked abruptly.

'It's past midnight,' said Marika.

7

ALICE AND LEO WALKED through the woods until the path split in two directions. There they turned right and followed the sign to the campsite.

'They might be using the camp as a retreat for confirmation students,' said Alice.

'Let's wait and see. If there are people around, we'll have to think of someplace else. Come on,' he said, tugging at her arm. They continued on as it began to drizzle. Alice thought it was lovely, with the rain cooling her face.

'Do you believe what your parents are saying?' she asked. 'That the world is about to end?'

'That's not what they're saying. They're just saying that climate change can no longer be stopped; in fact, it's escalating. And that's true. Just ask any climate scientist.'

'But what does it mean?'

'I don't think anybody knows the answer to that.'

'So do you agree with your parents? Do you want to do what they're doing?'

'You mean live primitively?'

'Is that what it's called?' asked Alice. She hadn't heard it described that way before.

'That's not what they're doing. I don't really understand what Pappa wants. I just hope that I'll be allowed to keep my mobile,' he said.

Alice laughed.

They had been walking for half an hour when they reached the campsite. They saw another sign and a narrower path. A couple of cars were parked nearby, but they didn't see anyone around.

'Shall we go over and find somewhere to sit?' asked Leo.

Alice nodded, so they headed into the camp area.

They saw a big red timbered house and a dozen cabins scattered along the shore. It was a beautiful place with granite rocks and a sandy beach, a volleyball net and a shore sauna.

Leo had brought a cloth bag filled with food, and Alice had her little loudspeaker. Her mobile had run out of juice, but Leo's phone had enough charge left to listen to music.

They walked to the cabin at the far end of the beach, hoping no one in the main building would notice them. The cabin was about the size of a small sauna hut, and when Leo tried the door, he found it unlocked.

'Bingo.'

'Do you think somebody is staying here?'

'Let's have a look.'

It seemed empty. There were mattresses and pillows on the beds, but no sheets or blankets. Pine needles covered the floor, and it looked as though no one had been there in a while. The air was raw and cold.

Leo sat down on one of the beds.

'Let's stay here. We have food and music. What more do we need?'

'Booze,' said Alice.

'Too bad we don't have any. Shall we take a look around the area?'

Leo brought his phone so they could listen to music as they walked.

A group of people dressed in white sat at a table on the big terrace of the main building. Leo went up to them, showing a curiosity that Alice lacked.

'Who are you?' he asked.

They looked strange, as if they were actors in some sort of theatre production. They all had the same old-fashioned hair-styles, and they wore what looked like old lab coats.

There were five of them, all about twenty-five years old, younger than Alice's parents, at any rate. They exchanged embarrassed looks.

'What are you kids doing here?' asked one of them. He had dark brown hair and a moustache, trimmed and waxed, the kind that might be seen in old photographs.

'We're just out taking a walk.'

'This is a private area. We've rented the whole place for the weekend,' said the man with the moustache.

'I think the beach is public property,' said Leo.

'We're in the middle of role-playing, so we'd appreciate it if you kids would leave us in peace. And turn that off,' he said, pointing at Leo's phone. 'You're wrecking the illusion. It's 1915 right now.'

'It's 2016,' said Leo.

'No, it's 1915, and we're at a sanatorium. Are you patients here? Do you want to be admitted to the hospital?'

Alice thought this whole thing seemed very strange. She'd never heard of anything like it. What were these people up to, anyway? Was it some kind of theatre?

'Sure,' said Leo with a shrug.

'Seriously?' said the man with the moustache.

'Leo, what's this all about?' asked Alice.

'If I understand it right, we're supposed to pretend to be sick and they're the doctors. Haven't you ever heard of role-playing?'

Alice shook her head.

'If you kids want to participate, you'll have to put on hospital clothes. We'll go and get them,' said the man.

One of the other young men, who was also wearing a doctor's white coat, seemed hesitant.

'But they're just kids. Should we really let them take part?'

'Why not?' asked the other man. 'Why shouldn't the hospital have kids with lung disease?'

They were each given a white cotton shirt and a pair of sweatpants, also white. They were escorted into the main building and told to lie down in white iron beds.

'In the daytime you're allowed out on the terrace. It's good for your health,' said a woman who belonged to the group. She had thick blond hair pinned up in a complicated style. It was a dreary place with a wood floor. Raw and cold. The lights were on and a fire was burning in the big fireplace.

There were other 'patients' as well, about ten in all. Leo and Alice whispered to each other, but the people playing doctors asked them to be quiet.

'No whispering. Not if you want to participate.'

They lay in separate beds for at least an hour. The sky grew dark and Alice regretted running away from home. She was just about to get up when someone came in to tell them it was time to eat. They were given beef broth with potatoes, carrots and leeks.

After the meal all the patients sat in a circle and talked. Mostly they talked about 'the war in Europe', which sounded sort of familiar to Alice from school, though she didn't really understand what they were saying. The mood was subdued, as if the others were immersed in thoughts that the world was about to end. Some of the 'patients' coughed and sniffled as they sat there.

Someone read aloud from a newspaper from 1915:

The Red Cross conference now taking place in Stockholm with delegates from Germany, Austria, Hungary and Russia has as its goal to ameliorate the harsh lot suffered by hundreds of thousands of prisoners of war. It is proof that the war has not stifled all sense of sympathy among those in power towards those unfortunate souls who are held captive.

Alice glanced at Leo, who was suppressing a grin. She had a hard time not laughing, and finally she started giggling uncontrollably. The others in the group gave her angry looks, and now Leo was also trying not to laugh.

'Children, do you think the news is funny?' asked one of the people playing a doctor.

'Not at all,' said Alice, giggling even more.

'We're going to put on a play later, and then you will be allowed to laugh and have fun. But right now we're discussing what's happening in the rest of Europe. Italy has just invaded Austria-Hungary, and no one knows what will happen next. Some people think there's going to be a big war, which will destroy us all,' said the doctor.

The others lowered their eyes and looked gloomy, but Leo stood up and took Alice's hand.

'Shall we go?'

She nodded.

They spent the rest of the evening on the beach, by themselves. Leo took pictures of Alice running along the water's edge.

They changed back into their own clothes and headed back to the cabin to eat the last of the food they'd brought along.

Sometime during the night they both fell asleep, and when Alice awoke the cabin was dark; she couldn't see a thing. Her arm had gone numb because they were lying so close together in the narrow bed, and she had a hard time remembering where she was.

'Leo, wake up!'

'Leo!' she whispered louder.

He opened his eyes. That was all she could see in the dark. His eyes.

'We fell asleep,' she said. 'We have to go home. I think it's awfully late.'

He sat up in bed.

'Fuck. I guess I was really tired. Which isn't so strange, since we've been spending every night texting each other,' he said.

Gradually her eyes grew accustomed to the dark, and she could see he was smiling at her. They hugged for a long time before getting up and leaving the cabin.

As they walked back along the road, Alice remembered the ring she'd found on the beach. It was in her pocket. She'd brought it along to show Leo, but then decided that would be a stupid, childish thing to do. Now she took it out.

'Would you like to have this?' she asked. 'Then you can remember me wherever you are.'

Leo stuck the ring on his thumb.

'That looks so cool,' he said.

8

WHEN IT STARTED RAINING in the morning, Kati moved the patio furniture inside. There was really no reason to do it, but she found it depressing to see everything out in the rain, and she decided not to wait until autumn to put the furniture away. The chairs and table weighed more than she'd expected, leaving deep tracks in the sand as she dragged them to the small woodshed behind the house. They were hard to fold, and she got a gash in the palm of her hand when she stowed away the large table. It was a deep cut, and blood ran down her arm as she walked across the yard to the house. She couldn't find any plasters, so she tore off a piece of paper towel and wrapped it around her hand.

She sat down by the window. The rain was coming down harder. She'd been here more than a hundred days now, never leaving the house except to cycle to the supermarket or – during the past few weeks – to spend time with Anders.

At least now she was eating decently. During the first months she'd merely eaten whatever was easiest. Ready-made meals, fruit, rye crispbread. When she was a student she'd eaten rye crispbread whenever she was short of money. All spring she'd found it oddly comforting to eat pieces of plain crispbread, without butter, as if that reminded her of when she and Johan were young and newly in love, living in a dormitory in Åbo.

Presumably she would have continued to eat that sort of food all summer – heating up whatever she had in the freezer, maybe going into town once in a while to buy wine – if her family, and later Anders, hadn't come to see her. She'd had a simple plan: to isolate herself from the world and simply stay here at the summer house until she was ready. But ready for what? She didn't really know, but she knew she needed time. That's what she was always telling her patients too: time heals all wounds. It was a cliché, of course, but clichés existed because they were true.

How long would it take?

In her work she often met people whose partners had left them, and it could take years for them to heal. They lost their appetite, had difficulty orienting themselves in their day-to-day lives, and were constantly losing or forgetting things. But ultimately almost everyone did recover.

It was worse for those whose partners had died. Or maybe it wasn't worse, but it was different.

Personally, she had nothing left.

Of course she had the children, but they were grown now and had their own lives.

She didn't even have the ring.

She'd been carrying it in her hand, not really knowing why, and suddenly it was gone. Like yet another sacrificial gift.

But then Anders had arrived. He was so awkward and fumbling at first, but he turned out to be a warm and kind person, and maybe he'd even helped her a little. It was as if she'd been waiting for him here all along, as if he was exactly what she needed. He'd acted as a therapist for her.

She didn't really understand what sort of relationship they had. Maybe they were just two people who needed to talk to each other. Two people who'd both ended up in a phase of their lives that made it necessary to retreat and leave the rest of the world outside.

But the more she talked, the more she noticed the past coming back. She was smart enough to realise that sooner or later she would have to work through her grief. She had never told any of her clients to lock themselves away in a summer house. But she had a hard time practicing what she preached.

It became too much for her. The grief was surging inside her chest, trying to escape, but she didn't want to burden Anders with her sorrow. She didn't want to force him to carry it too, yet she also knew that he wouldn't understand. What they had together couldn't sustain something like that. She was definitely not ready.

Grief took on strange forms. It ate through her like a worm, burrowing into her head until she felt completely hollowed out, and everything reminded her of her grief – everything she saw, everything she ate, everything she heard other people saying. She tried to avoid burdening him with all that.

Before Anders turned up she played tennis when she couldn't sleep. She would run around the court aggressively, slamming the ball against the green board as hard as she could.

She'd always played tennis with Johan. They'd played almost every day when they came out here to Mjölkviken. He'd taught her the sport, and she'd loved it – the feeling of having strong and sinewy calf muscles, of lunging freely across the asphalt. They taught the children to play too, and when they moved away from home, Kati and Johan continued their tennis games.

But Johan had gone skiing across the ice in April. There was nothing she could have done; she didn't even witness him falling through. She was in the city, and he'd come out here alone with the dog.

She still couldn't comprehend why he'd skied so far out.

After all these years he should have known that it was dangerous in April when the sun had been shining all day, making spots slushy and brittle. Under no circumstance should he have risked skiing there.

Maybe the problem was that Johan had been so experienced. Maybe he thought he could cope with anything. He'd talked about practicing for just such an event when he was serving in the military, how it was possible to crawl out on the ice using spikes. But presumably he hadn't thought about how hard it would be with skis and a big Siberian husky.

When they finally found him, there were signs that the dog had tried to get out before Johan, that Johan may have run into trouble because he was trying to save the dog. It was impossible to say, but Kati thought that's what must have happened. It would have been typical of him. That's the kind of person he was, always thinking of others.

All of his things were still back home in the city. She hadn't yet cleared anything away, and she'd withdrawn from everyone and everything. She'd asked for sick leave from her job, and then she'd come out here. She hadn't paid any bills or answered any phone calls except from the children.

In the beginning they had handled a lot of the practical matters, including the funeral arrangements and some of the paperwork, since she was too bereft to do it. But when that was taken care of, they went back to their own lives, as if nothing had happened. No, maybe not as if nothing had happened. But they had recovered considerably faster than she had, as if they were in a hurry to move on. She felt hurt by this, but she understood.

She and Anders tried to have sex today, for the first time, and it was clumsy and strange. She had to stop herself halfway through when she almost said 'I love you.' Instead, she said 'I love this.'

Anders hadn't managed to enter her because he wasn't hard enough. Afterwards they lay in bed and told each other it didn't matter, that maybe it had been a bad idea from the start. Maybe their relationship wasn't like this. Maybe it was about something else that had nothing to do with desire or sex but rather with other basic needs.

Anders got up to use the toilet. He was in the bathroom for a while and then flushed.

'What were you doing?' she asked.

'I flushed away the pills I brought from Hanoi. I don't need them.'

Julia dropped by an hour later to tell them the kids had disappeared, and Anders left to join the search. Kati stayed behind at the house, and for the first time she noticed how it really looked, how dirty and dreary it was, so she decided to do some cleaning.

9

THE KIDS CAME BACK HOME early in the morning. Anders and Julia had driven around half the night until they finally gave up. It wasn't until 3 a.m. that Anders realised they could check the kids' Instagram accounts, and that's when they saw that Leo had posted a picture of Alice on the beach. The picture was dark, but it had been posted only a couple of hours earlier.

'They're around here somewhere, so they're not in any danger. Maybe they just forgot they're children and there are certain rules they need to follow,' said Anders.

'I thought she might pull something like this sooner or later,' said Julia. 'I'm glad mobile phones exist, but I'm also annoyed that we can't get hold of them.'

Julia had fallen asleep in the car. Anders had to wake her and lead her up to the summer house. She didn't want to go to bed, so she sat on the terrace to wait until morning. At that point she was planning to ring the police. She was relieved that Alice seemed to be alive, but she wanted her daughter home.

At five in the morning Alice came walking up to the house. It was still barely light, the sort of summertime darkness that is quiet and contained. The sky began rumbling ominously, and Alice was wet and tired from the walk.

'Where have you two been?' asked Julia. She was no longer angry, merely relieved, as if operating on adrenaline. She'd had three cups of coffee and everything seemed unreal: the muted low pressure system, the impending thunder – and Alice, who seemed so happy even though her lips were blue.

At no point had Julia felt truly frantic. She suspected that Alice had gone somewhere with Leo, and that neither of them was in any serious danger. There was very little traffic in the area, and for both of them to have drowned was such an appalling thought that she hadn't even fully considered the possibility.

Alice changed her clothes and fell asleep on the sofa in the living room.

Julia also slept for a few hours. When she awoke it was already eleven in the morning and it was raining heavily. Anton was awake, sitting in the kitchen. Julia started making breakfast as she phoned her parents. Her father answered.

'Are you alone?' she asked.

'Yes, your mother went to the supermarket,' replied Göran.

'Oh.'

For a moment neither of them spoke.

'Pappa?'

'Yes, dear?'

'What do you know about Mamma and Sten Segerkvist?'

A long silence.

'Pappa?' Julia repeated.

'Why are you asking me that?'

'Because I saw Marika, and she started talking about a lot of …'

'Do you really want to know?'

'What is there to know?'

'Hmm … Well, I suppose it doesn't matter any more.'

'So tell me.'

'It was a long time ago. They had an affair that lasted for several years, every summer when we were in Mjölkviken. At least a couple of summers. I didn't know anything about it until after it was over. Do you remember the time when we talked about getting a divorce?'

'Yes. Mamma talked about it a lot, but you didn't.'

'That was after I read the letters.'

'What letters?'

'They wrote to each other all the time, during the winter, planning how they were going to leave their spouses and start a new life together. There was a whole box of their letters.'

'I didn't know that.'

'Of course you didn't.'

'But nothing happened, right? I mean, they didn't leave.'

'Fortunately. He was a handsome man, a doctor, but a bloody idiot, if you ask me. A real ladies' man who promised her the moon. Finally her friends talked sense into her.'

'So that's why you bought the summer house closer to the city? That's why you don't come out here any more?'

'Well, there are other reasons too. I think it's more pleasant to be closer to town. But that was certainly one of the reasons. That place has negative associations for me.'

After talking to her father, Julia rang Erik. Outside there was a real downpour, with lightning flashing in the kitchen windows. It was eerie, almost frightening. The storm seemed to be centred right above the summer house.

'Hi, sweetheart,' she said.

She could tell at once that something was wrong. Erik's voice sounded odd, as if he didn't know how to begin.

'There's something I have to tell you,' he said.

All sorts of things raced through her mind – that he'd met someone else, that he'd been in an accident, that he'd found himself in the drunk tank, that he realised he was gay.

The last thing she would have imagined was that he'd been sacked.

'So there's nothing to be done about it at the moment,' he said. 'I'll try to find a new job in the autumn.'

'Did you just find out about this?'

'I've known since midsummer, but I didn't want to say anything. I don't know why. I suppose I thought I'd be able to find another job and then you wouldn't have to worry.'

Another lightning flash. Only a few seconds later a thunderous boom, like a huge explosion, directly overhead. Julia jumped. Anton looked scared.

'My God,' said Julia.

'We'll be okay.'

'It's not that,' she said. 'We're having a thunderstorm here. A really big one.'

She placed her hand on the worktop and leaned forward.

'But I'll be getting a severance package,' Erik went on. 'So we'll be able to manage for at least six months.'

Julia nodded, as another flash of lightning lit up the room, followed by an even louder crack of thunder.

'Erik, I'm starting to feel scared.'

'It's just thunder.'

'I know, but it seems to be right on top of us. Isn't there an old TV antenna on the roof that the lightning could strike?'

'It's very unlikely that would happen. But you could go sit in the car. That's what we always did when I was little.'

Julia glanced at Anton.

'Okay, Erik. I've got to go now.'

'I talked to Martin,' he said. 'I thought he might have something for me.'

'How did it go?'

'That's the worst part. Even his company is cutting back. There's just nothing right now.'

'How strange,' she said.

'I think so too. Julia?'

'Yes?'

'Do you love me?'

'Oh,' she said.

'What is it?' asked Erik.

'More lightning.'

The instant she said that, thunder boomed with such force that it felt as if the whole house might be split in two.

'Mamma?' said Anton.

Julia looked at him.

'Erik, I need to go. I love you.'

'Okay,' he said. 'Take care of yourselves.'

She ended the call and set her mobile on the table. Then she glanced at Anton, who now looked really scared.

'Is Alice still asleep?' she asked.

'I think so,' said Anton.

'She must be tired. Shall we go sit in the car and wait for the storm to pass?'

They ran out to the car through the rain. When they were inside, Julia switched on the radio. She thought about Alice still in the house, and she wondered if they should wake her. But she wanted to hide out in the safe confines of the car, mostly for her own sake. They sat there for half an hour until the thunder finally moved on, like an unwelcome guest. When the rain started to let up Julia opened the car door. Anton got out and walked down to the road.

Big streams of water were running down the road towards the ditch. Anton knelt down and began making little canals that led to bigger furrows. He created a big, complex system of channels for the water. He wasn't bothered by the fact that it was still raining because it was warm outside. He wanted to be alone to think and to take in everything through his senses.

He had just dug a new furrow when he caught sight of Marika. She walked past him, as stiff as a zombie in a horror film. She looked upset, as if she were walking in her sleep and dreaming about something scary.

Anton froze as she walked past. He didn't know what to do. 'Hello?' he said.

But she didn't respond as she simply continued on.

Then someone came running. The thin man with the dreadlocks. Anton didn't know his name. He was carrying a blanket. He rushed forward and wrapped the blanket around Marika.

Only then did she stop. Anton could see that she was hurt. Her forehead was bleeding, and her legs were muddy, maybe from falling.

'How are you?' asked the man.

'Don't worry,' she said. 'I'll be fine. Wait ... where am I?'

'You're walking along the road. I tried to stop him, but he hit me. I'm sorry,' he said.

'Who are you?'

'Ville,' he said. 'Don't you recognise me?'

'Ah,' she said. She looked down at her body and saw that she was naked under the blanket.

'Why don't I have any clothes on?' she asked.

'I don't know,' said Ville.

10

ALL SUMMER LONG MARIKA had been afraid to wake up each morning, afraid that Chris would be irritable and capricious, afraid that he would threaten her or do something unpredictable. Maybe he'd take Leo and run off to Scotland or God only knew where, without saying a word to her.

She'd been sleeping on the sofa for the past three weeks, ever since Helena moved into their bedroom. Chris wanted all three of them to sleep in the same bed, but that was too much for Marika. Instead she lay awake at night, listening to them panting. She heard Helena's moans, her animal-like howling, and Chris's repeated commands, telling Helena to get down on all fours, or telling her to suck his dick. Marika could hear everything that went on in the house, and she could understand why Leo had moved out to the yurt and later taken Alice along to the woods.

This was not a good environment for children, no matter what Chris might think.

She no longer remembered when it all started. In the beginning he'd been so wonderful and tender, so different from all the men she'd previously known. The special upbringing that he'd had seemed to lend a certain melancholy to his face. And it gave him a genuine curiosity about everything in nature, from the tiniest bug to the big topographical changes at various places they'd visited over the years. She had a feeling that no topic was too big or difficult for Chris to tackle, and he always shared his views with her. It was like being with someone who was constantly moving forward, who wanted life to be one big adventure, who could *make* life into one big adventure. That was what it was like when they visited Death Valley in the States, when they explored caves in Australia, and when they went surfing near Lofoten.

But then his behaviour changed. Small things at first. Like the times he'd get angry if she made friends with people and wanted to go see them. She remembered when they were living in Edinburgh and she decided she wanted to study psychology. In the beginning he was enthusiastic, but when she actually enrolled in classes and was away from home in the daytime, he got more and more surly. He showed less interest in what she told him, and finally he flew into a rage when she decided to join a study group that met on Tuesday evenings.

Shortly afterwards they moved out to a house he'd found for them, a place with sheep and chickens and dog kennels, which meant they both had to work from morning to night, while Marika also had to manage Leo's homeschooling. And then all sorts of people started turning up. Poets and authors whose work had been published by small literary houses or who had self-published their writing on blogs; musicians who travelled around Europe, living a nomadic life, but always finding new families or couples who would offer them room and board.

Marika heard amazing stories and met some marvellous people – there was absolutely nothing wrong with most of them – but she never had any time to herself. She was always expected to offer hospitality to the steady stream of people who turned up on their doorstep and who Chris would inevitably invite in.

Soon there were women too. The more serious Chris grew about his de-civilisation ideas, the more he insisted that monogamy was unnatural, that an exclusive relationship between two people was a modern invention. If they were going to take the movement seriously, then they ought to explore all forms of non-civilisation and break with the nuclear family norm. For him this became an obsession. He said he wanted to de-civilise himself, and that meant obeying his animal impulses.

Soon twenty-two-year-old girls turned up from Macedonia, and thirty-year-old women from Copenhagen, and married couples who wanted to try out the swinger lifestyle of trading sexual partners and everything else in between. Chris walked around like a horny patriarch in a family of Mormons, and Marika began thinking more and more about leaving him.

She had hoped that spending the summer in Mjölkviken would give her family some peace and quiet. She was starting to worry about Leo and how all this might be affecting him.

She hadn't imagined that Chris would be able to entice so many people to her old summer house in Mjölkviken. She thought it would seem too far away from the rest of the world, and the Aniara movement had no foothold in Finland.

Yet it didn't take long before the first visitors turned up. And one day Chris announced that he'd invited a Greek woman named Helena to their summer house. He explained that he'd also paid for her plane ticket because of the difficult economic situation in Greece. He didn't know how long she would stay.

It was Chris's money. Marika had nothing to say about how it was spent. She'd never had access to his bank account, and she had no idea how much money he had, but she realised he must have a sizeable amount. It was money he had earned during his university days and afterwards when he worked in finance. Chris never talked about himself, but she'd heard about all this from some of his old friends, with whom they'd been in contact at the beginning of their relationship. Chris was no longer in touch with anyone from his former life. New people were always turning up, and this was also something he managed to explain with his home-grown psychological theories about evolution. He said that in reality human beings were hunter-gatherers and had basically always wandered. 'How do you think humans ever managed to leave Africa if they weren't perennially curious about nature?' he asked Marika whenever she questioned why they couldn't stay in one place longer than six months.

She heard Chris and Helena getting up and going into the kitchen. Helena was in the habit of walking around the house dressed only in a T-shirt and knickers. Marika hated that. She hated the sassy, casual way Helena moved.

She had decided to voice her objections. Things could no longer go on like this. She wanted a more normal life, a healthier and simpler life that would be better suited for Leo. She no longer wanted to have to light fires at night or smoke hash or speak in tongues down at the beach.

She went into the kitchen and found Chris and Helena sitting at the table.

'I want her to go home now,' she said.

'Who?' asked Chris.

'Helena. I want her to go home. The others have already left, and I want my family back. Or else I'm going to leave and take Leo with me.'

Chris stared at his plate with a smile on his face.

'Not everybody has left. Ville is still here. And Helena.'

'But I want them to leave.'

'So that's the way it is?'

'That's the way it is,' replied Marika, though she could hear the hesitation in her voice. She thought about all the times her own mother had stood up to her father, and how frightening that had always felt. In the long run it had been pointless, leading only to screaming, hitting and crying.

'Let me tell you one thing,' said Chris. 'In this house I make my own decisions. And I want Helena to stay. If you're not happy with that, you're free to leave. But you're not taking Leo with you.'

'Oh yes I am,' she said.

Chris stood up so abruptly that his chair scraped against the floor. Marika flinched, noticing how scared she was of him, how scared she was that he would assault her.

But he merely left the room.

For a long moment Helena and Marika simply stared at each other without speaking. Marika thought she saw a trace of doubt, maybe even fear, in Helena's eyes.

She heard Chris go into the bedroom, pause, and then start rummaging in the chest of drawers.

When he came back, he was carrying a rope.

11

MARIKA DIDN'T RECOGNISE VILLE until he told her his name. She began to shiver when she realised she was naked, so she wrapped the blanket tighter around her body.

'Where is Chris?' she asked.

'I left him back at the house with Helena. Don't worry, he's not going anywhere. Maybe we should ring for an ambulance. I hit him awfully hard.'

Now it all came back to her. Chris had threatened to tie her up with the rope. At first Marika thought he was joking. But then she provoked him by calling him a loser and saying she wanted to leave him. She said she hated him and hoped he'd have a happy life with Helena. That's when he rushed at her and put her in a choke-hold. Marika had managed to break free from his grip, but on her way out of the kitchen she collided with the stove and got a big gash on her knee.

Marika then ran out of the house, but she was slowed down by the wound on her knee. Chris came after her and grabbed hold of her so she fell to the sand, with him on top of her, knocking the breath out of her. He was strong and heavy and there was no way she'd be able to sit up. She got sand in her mouth and her knee stung. As he tore the clothes off her, his grip suddenly loosened. Now she realised it was because Ville had seen everything and had launched himself at Chris. Ville had saved her.

Anton was sitting next to the wet road, looking at them.

'Go get your mother,' said Ville. 'Hurry up.'

The summer house in Mjölkviken stood on a foundation that was nearly a metre high. When Anton came running towards the house he noticed that water was running out from underneath the cellar door. The door was old and worn, made of rough boards and stained the same colour as the rest of the house. The water was coming out of the narrow gap between the ground and the door. There was a sewage drain right outside the cellar door, but that didn't seem to help. The water was rising so fast that Anton could imagine it spreading across the whole yard, a pool of water that would keep getting bigger and bigger.

He didn't really know what to say to his mother. Maybe she wouldn't even believe him.

By now he'd grown accustomed to the summer house. He no longer thought it smelled strange. In fact, he actually liked how the varnished floorboards felt under his feet, a hard surface that nevertheless possessed a certain softness, so that it felt especially nice walking barefoot. And the air inside the house was no longer as raw or damp as when they'd arrived. The house had been warmed by their bodies and by the living-room fireplace, where Julia often lit a fire. And the bedroom, which was where he now headed, was a real bedroom, with Julia sitting in the bed and reading, the covers pulled over her.

'Mamma, Marika got hurt and needs help.'

She stared at him.

'What?'

'Down on the road. She's naked.'

After his mother took off running, Anton sat outside for a long time, looking at the steady stream of water running into the yard.

12

LEO CAME OVER AFTER Julia drove Marika to the hospital to get checked out. She hadn't suffered any serious injuries, but when the police came to arrest Chris and interview Marika, who agreed to file charges against him, they suggested that she go into town to have a doctor look at her knee.

Anton had listened to the grown-ups talking and understood that for some reason Chris had attacked Marika, but Ville had saved her. Anton had heard only portions of what the grown-ups were saying, but clearly nobody had died. He still couldn't understand why Marika had not been wearing any clothes.

When Julia came back from town, she discovered the water gushing out from under the cellar door.

Although maybe 'gushing' wasn't really the right word. The water was slowly rising and spreading across the yard, running down towards the sauna building. The water was not clear. It was brown and slightly sludgy, about the same as the stagnant water in the tarn. It smelled of sewage, and it stained the lawn and rocks brown.

Julia put on her rubber boots and opened the cellar door. Even before she could turn on the light, she could see there was water everywhere, turning the whole floor into a shiny black pool. When the light was on, she realised the water was at least half a metre deep. It was a brownish-black colour with patches of petrol or oil lending a silvery gleam to the surface.

The water didn't seem to be rising quickly, but Julia did the first thing that came to mind, which was to grab a broom from a corner of the room and try to find the drain so she could sweep away any leaves that might be acting as a plug.

The problem was that she couldn't see anything. Even if she located the drain, which should be in the centre of the room, there was too much water for her to see whether it was blocked or not.

'Everything is falling apart here. I need to ring Grandpa. Or somebody,' she said as she came into the house.

But then she thought about phoning Anders instead. He had helped out when Alice went missing, and he'd seemed happy to be of use. He had offered her comfort when she was feeling desperate.

Anders was at the beach when he took the call.

'Could you come over and have a look at something?' she asked him. 'We'll probably have to get a plumber to come out.'

'I'll be right there.'

Anders stood in the cellar as Julia shone a pocket torch at the pipes so he'd be able to see. Alice and Leo had also come down to the cellar to find out what was going on. Leo was pensive and subdued, and Alice felt sorry for him. Marika was supposed to come home from the hospital later in the day.

'On first glance it doesn't look as if the pipes are leaking. The water could be seeping up from the ground. The pipes might have burst during the winter,' he said.

'But why is the water brown? It doesn't seem to be sewage water. It looks more like murky sea water.'

'That puzzles me too.'

Julia stood in the cellar thinking that the strange smell down here was almost blatantly symbolic and Freudian.

'I don't think there's much I can do,' said Anders.

'Maybe I should phone my father,' said Julia.

'But it doesn't seem to be getting any deeper. Or is that just my imagination?'

Anders was right. The water now seemed to be standing still. No matter where it had come from, it seemed to have stopped rising.

'Isn't Erik back yet?' asked Anders.

Julia shook her head. 'Would you like some coffee?' she asked.

Later that afternoon a plumber arrived at the summer house along with Julia's father. They spent an hour in the cellar, trying to gain access to the drain so the water could run out. They emerged from the cellar, hauling out big piles of brown sludge that had come out of the ground.

When they finally managed to locate the problem, they were able to stop the flow of water.

'I can't explain it any other way except to tell you that somehow the water from the tarn was running out from under the house,' said the plumber. 'It's not sewer water. It smells different. Not exactly pleasant, but fresher. And there's vegetation in the water, which indicates it must have come from some water source near the house. You should probably have a thorough inspection done.'

Julia's father sighed.

'Damn it all. I suspected something was rotting, but I thought it was because the pipes were old or the foundations had started to crumble. And, to be honest, I wouldn't have minded if the whole house fell apart. We never come out here any more, and it would be impossible to sell a house that can't pass inspection.'

13

THERE WAS A HINT OF AUTUMN in the air as the children put their suitcases in the car. Julia was looking at the house, thinking it was a shame to leave now that the summer had wrapped itself around her shoulders and the sea was finally warm.

The seasons of the year made her think about death. There was an inescapable melancholy linked to the end of the summer holidays.

Erik had phoned earlier in the morning. He wanted to stay in Helsinki because he was trying to sort out his job situation. That was fine with her. They would talk when she got home. Or maybe they wouldn't. She wasn't yet sure.

Anders had promised to ride with them to Helsinki.

'I can't stay here. Kati needs to go back to the city to see her kids. It wouldn't be good for her to stay here all autumn,' he said.

Anders went to Kati's to say goodbye while Julia waited in the yard. Julia had hoovered the whole house using an old vacuum cleaner she'd found in the attic. When she cleaned the front hall she'd caught a glimpse of herself in the mirror and almost flinched. She found it hard to accept that she was actually that person looking back at her. A woman who would soon turn thirty-six and who had apparently gone through some sort of mild depression, or maybe it was a completely ordinary case of writer's block.

She thought about that as she cleaned the house, about how unnecessary it was. Nobody felt happier if she went around stewing in her own hopelessness. She needed to roll up her sleeves and pull herself out of it. She should finish writing her novel instead of wandering about like some restless ghost, with an unspecified sense of dissatisfaction.

She raised her arms and stretched, easing the muscles in the back of her neck. This autumn would be better than last year's.

Anton came into the house.

'Mamma?'

'Yes, sweetie?'

'Do you think we'll come back here next summer?'

Julia looked at him.

'I don't know. Would you like that?'

Anton thought for a moment.

'I could come back. It's a nice place.'

Julia nodded.

'Sure, we can come back.'

Julia drove the first part of the way. She preferred to take the small roads in Ostrobothnia because that was less stressful than the highway between Tammerfors and Helsinki. They listened to the radio. On the news they heard that the month of July had been the hottest since the first records were kept back in the 1800s.

'They're probably right, you know,' said Anders. 'Chris and the others, I mean. I have no doubt that the climate is going to hell. And just like they said, there's not much we can do about it.'

Anton leaned forward from the back seat.

'Mamma? Do you think we're going to see the end of the world?'

Julia turned around to look at him.

'I don't know. Probably not the end of the world, but you may see a lot of big changes happening on earth during your lifetime. With refugees arriving from different countries. And it's going to get warmer in Finland,' said Julia.

She looked out at the yellow fields, at the flat acres, and the typical barns of Ostrobothnia.

They had driven past Nykarleby, and a tractor was now moving slowly on the road ahead of them. Julia accelerated to pass it, not noticing the oncoming vehicle until it was too late. She had to swerve to avoid hitting the car.

'Julia!' shouted Anders. 'What the hell are you doing?'

'Sorry,' she said, thinking they hadn't been in any danger, even though it might have seemed as if they were. There was plenty of room on the road, and the other car had also veered to the side. It might have looked dramatic, but they'd been perfectly safe inside the car the whole time.